The Education of Pip

The Education of Pip

By
Sarah Wallace

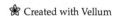

For those who keep learning, growing, and teaching themselves difficult lessons:
this book is for you.

CONTENTS

Content Warning   ix

Chapter 1   1
Chapter 2   9
Chapter 3   17
Chapter 4   27
Chapter 5   40
Chapter 6   49
Chapter 7   58
Chapter 8   69
Chapter 9   77
Chapter 10   87
Chapter 11   97
Chapter 12   104
Chapter 13   113
Chapter 14   121
Chapter 15   128
Chapter 16   140
Chapter 17   148
Chapter 18   154
Chapter 19   163
Chapter 20   170
Note from the Author   179
Acknowledgments   181
About the Author   183
Also by Sarah Wallace   185
Preview for Letters to Half Moon Street   189
Preview for One Good Turn   196
Sign up for my newsletter!   204
Preview for The Glamour Spell of Rose Talbot   205

CONTENT WARNING

The Education of Pip continues the story of Pip Standish from *One Good Turn*. As such there are some darker themes explored in this story.

My books will always be about the power of kindness and hope and will always have a HEA, but please note that this book includes the following:

- references to a past abusive relationship (including grooming and sex trafficking)
- a scene with on-page assault
- depression
- characters who have chosen sex work

CHAPTER 1

PHILIP STANDISH SAT HUNCHED in a cell. His knees were pulled up to his chest and he was clasping his elbows, making himself as small as possible. Since he was a petite man, this wasn't exactly difficult. He had so far evaded the notice and interest of his cell mates, but as he was generally considered a pretty sort of person—with faun-colored skin, dark eyes with long lashes, curly hair, and pouting lips—he did not know how long he would remain unnoticed, and he didn't like to depend too heavily on luck.

He was unsurprised to be there, which was a little unsettling to realize. Considering he'd learned to pickpocket at a very young age, prison had always loomed as a grisly possibility.

Philip, or Pip, as everyone called him, had never known his parents. One of many orphans wandering the streets of London, he had been picked up by Jack Reid when he was barely old enough to talk. While in Jack's care, Pip met Nell Birks, a tall, burly girl who came to be his best friend and most stalwart protector.

Nell knew her place was not among the dingy back alleys of London, sneaking around and picking pockets. But Pip knew his place too. And his place was where he had always been: in Jack's hands—both figuratively and literally. Sitting in a dark cell felt right too, in a strange sort of way.

When Pip was little, Jack taught him how to pick pockets, how to sneak about the alleyways, how to run from the constable. As Pip grew older and prettier, Jack taught him how to turn on the charm to dazzle the unsuspecting wealthy as he stole their purses. Later, Jack taught him how to pick locks and filch from more than just pockets. When Nell left Jack's employ to find honest work for herself, Pip found himself lonelier than he had ever been. Which is when Jack taught him a very new sort of lesson, one that involved heated kisses and long, stroking touches.

Pip owed Jack his life and it was a debt he could never repay. Which was why, later, when Jack sat him down and explained very calmly and clearly that the time had come for Pip to pay back his debt in a different manner, he knew better than to complain.

Jack started walking him to Covent Garden and sending him home with other men, wealthy men who gave him long, lingering looks and handed Jack their money in advance. Laid out on plush mattresses, kneeling on fine carpets, and then sent away before the sun came up, Pip concluded the shame he now felt for his own face and body was yet another lesson he was meant to learn from Jack. Jack had seamlessly changed Pip's beauty from a weapon to be used on unsuspecting marks to one leveraged against Pip himself. With every stranger's look of interest, Pip felt his worth diminish.

The first person to make him feel otherwise was Viscount Finlington. Like many people, Lord Finlington had been taken with Pip's looks and hadn't attempted to hide it. But the viscount had been so casual in his flirtations that Pip suspected he was like that to everybody. It made the gentleman's compliments feel less pointed and, for some strange reason, Pip appreciated that. He appreciated it even more when the viscount rejected Jack's offer of an evening spent with Pip.

They had met the viscount at the Fox & Thistle and Jack had pitched it in his usual way. He had cupped Pip's chin with one hand and stroked Pip's hair with the other and said, "He is a treat for the eyes, isn't he? And so sweet to touch. Would you like to try him for the night? I can assure you he's worth the price."

Then Jack wound fingers around some of Pip's curls and gave a little tug, drawing a small gasp from his lips. It was a constant source of embarrassment to Pip that he never failed to gasp when Jack tugged his hair during an offer. He suspected Jack changed little things—the placement, the intensity, the angle, the timing—so as to always produce a genuine reaction. It was those little involuntary gasps that made every customer's expression turn from interest to lust.

Until Lord Finlington. The viscount had surprised him. He had leveled Jack with a look so direct as to seem uncharacteristic and said, "Charming as that notion might be, my man, I never accept propositions from third parties. Now, if that concludes our business, I must be off. Pip, darling, it was a pleasure as ever to see you. Please give my regrets to dear Nell that I could not stay to bid her good evening." With that, the gentleman left.

Pip thought of the conversation and the viscount often. He didn't quite understand Lord Finlington's wording and Jack never explained it to him. He spent many nights wondering if the viscount's answer would have been the same if Pip had been at liberty to offer himself up. He would give in to certain flights of fancy—wondering what the viscount's lips would feel like on his skin, wondering what it would be like exploring the other man's body with his own lips and hands. Sometimes when Jack took him to bed, Pip would close his eyes and imagine it was Lord Finlington undressing him instead. He would imagine those touches to be reverent rather than proprietary. It was a pitiful and useless sort of revenge, but it had sweetened many a sour night since.

After Nell left permanently to learn magic from the viscount, Pip would often sneak off to Berkeley Square and look longingly at the one address that he knew housed a kind soul. Then he'd slink back to Jack's bed and allow Jack to comfort him, as Jack always did after a night spent with someone else, all the while wishing the comfort was coming from a different source.

He dug the heels of his palms into his eyes, trying to blot out thoughts of the elegant viscount. A boot kicked the sole of his foot and he looked up warily. A guard stood over him, holding a small lantern.

"You Standish?" the guard said gruffly.

Pip nodded.

"Come on then."

Confused and frightened, Pip followed the guard out of the cell, ignoring the curious looks of his fellow prisoners. Were they going to hang him already?

He was escorted to another small cell that had a table and two chairs. In one of those chairs sat Lord Finlington. Older than Pip, but significantly younger than Jack, he was a man of average height and round figure, pale skin, brown hair several shades lighter than Pip's own, a perpetual upward tilt to his well-shaped mouth, and lovely grey eyes. He was utterly beautiful but wore his beauty more comfortably than Pip had ever worn his, being neither self-deprecating nor self-congratulatory about it.

He was dressed, as usual, in the finest attire Pip had ever seen; a dark green traveling outfit, perfectly polished boots, a crisp cravat, and a long velvet cloak with a matching hat. He held a dark wood walking stick, the top covered in gold filigree, and was tapping it against the ground with rhythmic absentmindedness.

He stood up as Pip entered and grinned broadly. "Pip, darling, so good to see you again. Do, please take a seat."

The cell door clicked shut, but Pip noticed with interest that it was not locked. He sat down as Lord Finlington asked. The viscount appeared pleased as ever to see him, but Pip felt self-conscious to be found in a prison cell by the man he had recently come to idolize.

"I do apologize for not coming to chat with you sooner, my friend. You see, I was not aware of your change in address until yesterday afternoon. Dear Nell learned about it and informed me at once. I hope you are well, m'dear, considering," he said, his eyes darting over Pip as if assuring himself of Pip's safety.

Pip thought "change of address" a remarkably delicate way of putting his current situation. He didn't know if he was more amused or embarrassed by the unique turn of phrase.

"I am, sir, thank you," he said.

"Good," Lord Finlington said, relaxing a little. "I hoped as much. Now, you are probably wondering why I am here at all. As much as I love to keep people in suspense, I will simply get straight to the point. Do you mind?"

Pip frowned at the odd question and shook his head.

"Excellent," the viscount said. "I have spoken to Sir Alfred Bamble. He's a decent sort of chap, very proper, very sensible. He's a friend of mine and he also happens to be a judge, you see. I had him over for dinner last night and had a nice long chat with the gentleman. Although it is frightfully rude to talk about people who aren't present, I hope you won't be offended, Pip dear, that we talked about you a great deal." He paused, as if waiting for Pip to comment. When Pip didn't, the viscount continued, "We have come to an agreement, Sir Alfred and I. He has agreed that you might be given a second chance. That is to say, he has agreed to release you from your sentence, but he has some terms."

Pip sat up straighter.

"I am sure you will understand that Sir Alfred is a tiny bit concerned with your fascinating history. He admitted to some suspicion that were you to be released, you would simply return to your old life and your old career, and of course, your old associates."

Pip started to feel a mixture of relief and panic. Lord Finlington had clearly arranged for his release, but Pip knew nothing outside of his life with Jack. He had no training, no experience, and certainly no acquaintances. He waited for the viscount to continue, clenching his hands together in his lap, his heart hammering.

"I have offered a solution to Sir Alfred's concerns that I think will satisfy him and will help tidy up several problems I have observed. I have a dear friend, Miss Hartford, a lovely lady who has taken over a spell shop in a little town in Bedfordshire, if you can believe it, darling. I haven't been there yet, m'self, but I've been told it is a quaint little place, surrounded by lovely countryside. I believe the girl might actually be a genius, but there are limits, sadly, to what she can accomplish on her own. She was not, you understand, brought up to work in trade, so it has been an exciting new experience for her. As I understand it, running a shop is a great deal more work than she anticipated. I daresay she's up to the challenge, but I think a little help might be called for. I suggested to Sir Alfred that you might be precisely what is wanted in this matter. And Sir Alfred has agreed that if I see you to Miss Hartford's shop and accept personal responsibility for your redemption, as it were, then he will allow you to leave today."

Pip was stunned. Not only that the viscount had thought everything through so carefully, but that he had cared enough to do so. Who was Pip to receive such treatment? There was also a small, niggling worry that there might be an unspoken condition in terms of his release. He thought carefully before replying.

"That is really very kind of you, sir," he said at last. "I cannot tell you how grateful I am. I have some questions, if you do not think it too impertinent?"

Lord Finlington smiled. "Glad to do it, darling. Please ask as many questions as you like."

Pip took a deep breath. "What will my duties be? I've never...worked in trade either."

"That is a superb question, m'dear. I confess I do not know the intricacies of shop life, m'self. But I suspect your duties will have something to do with overall cleanliness of the shop, organizing the wares, assisting Miss Hartford with any heavy lifting, keeping an eye on the shop front while she is working in the back. That sort of thing. Would that suit?"

"I think so, sir, but does Miss Hartford know of this?" Pip asked. "I mean, does she know about me?"

Lord Finlington's smile deepened. "Yes, sweet thing, she knows. Or, I should say, she will. I sent word ahead to her, giving her the particulars. From what I know of Miss Hartford, I can assure you that she will be delighted to have your acquaintance and your assistance."

Pip wasn't entirely sure he believed this. It still seemed too good to be true. "That all sounds very fine, sir," he said. He hesitated. "Might I ask if there are any...other conditions that I don't yet know about, in terms of my release?"

The viscount's smile turned sympathetic. "None, Pip. You will have your own room somewhere nearby. I have yet to sort out that particular detail, I'm afraid. Although I imagine you will stay with Charlie. Do you remember Charlie, dear? He was at my house on the evening we met. Tall chap, devastatingly handsome? Anyway, he is engaged to Miss Hartford's adorable brother, and as both Hartfords are staying with him, I expect that he will extend the same invitation to you. At least until accommodations can be arranged for your long-term residence elsewhere. That way you can learn from Miss Hartford all the time, as it were. There will also be another party staying at the house for a little while, the Dukex of Molbury. They are a relation of mine, actually, but they are staying with Charlie as a chaperone. I like to think their presence will add to your peace of mind, for they will be ensuring propriety is maintained throughout the house. Oh, and you will not be working for Miss Hartford for free, of course; I will see to your salary. I'm a patron of sorts for the shop."

Pip studied the gentleman's face, searching for unsaid words, for traps, for expectations. Finding none of these things, he said, "I don't know how I shall ever repay you, sir."

The viscount stood, tapping his walking stick against the ground as he did so. "There is no need, darling, I assure you. I am always happy to help my friends. I hope that we can be friends?" he said, holding his hand out.

Pip shook it. "Yes, sir." He added with a small smile, "I suppose I might count you as such ever since you chose not to turn me in for breaking into your house."

Lord Finlington threw back his head with a laugh. "Splendid! I am thrilled to hear it, darling. Now, let us be off. I hope you don't mind, but I believe it might be best if we go straight to Tutting-on-Cress at this juncture. Come along, dear."

And with that, he led the way out of the cell and out of the building.

CHAPTER 2

LORD FINLINGTON HAD a carriage waiting on the street outside. Pip hardly had occasion to ride in carriages, except when Jack sent him home with someone. In those cases, he never sat alone, as he was always held close in another man's arms or lap. So there had been little opportunity to revel in the experience.

Lord Finlington insisted Pip sit in the front-facing seat and had taken the seat opposite. So, for the first time, Pip had the chance to look out the window and feel a little grand about being driven around.

It took them nearly an hour just to get outside London. He was so disoriented from the sensation that he mustered up the courage to ask how far away Tutting-on-Cress was. The viscount chuckled at the question and assured him they would arrive in time for dinner.

Once on the country road, Lord Finlington had the carriage pull over. He got out, taking his walking stick with him.

"We're not there already, sir?" Pip asked.

"Heavens no, darling. I'm just going to do a little speed spell to shorten the trip." He paused, looking back at Pip in the coach. "Would you like to watch?"

Pip scrambled out before the viscount could change his mind. He had never seen magic done before, not really. That is, he had watched Nell do a handful of spells, but she had admitted that she knew little of what she was doing, and, besides, her spells had only worked some of the time.

He watched in awe as the viscount pulled a drawstring bag from his pocket and took a large silk handkerchief out of it. He carefully set the handkerchief on the dirt road. Next, he plucked a compass out of the bag and set it on the handkerchief, then placed his own gold pocket watch next to the compass. Finally came a feather and a letter opener. He handed the feather and the empty bag to Pip, asking him to hold them. Pip did, gingerly pinching the feather shaft between his thumb and forefinger.

The viscount squatted and inscribed a few symbols onto the ground with the blade of the letter opener. Then he stood and dragged his walking stick along the ground, circling the coach, the horses, and the small pile of items. When he completed the circle, he beckoned Pip to come closer.

Pointing his walking stick at the watch, he said, "That is to ensure we make good time. That," he said, letting the walking stick tap the handkerchief, "is to provide comfort for the horses. Keep in mind, m'dear, when you are doing a spell that involves animals, that you look to the animal's comfort. The compass is a detail so we don't get lost. It isn't strictly necessary, mind, but magic can be a finicky thing. I feel it is always good to remember the details."

He waved the walking stick over the symbols scraped into the road, careful not to touch or smudge them. "This is the written portion of the spell, you see. The circle around the coach and the spell dictates what is included in the spell, while the inscription anchors it all together and specifies what the magic in the spell is meant to do. Now, for the feather," he said, holding out his hand.

Pip placed it carefully in his palm.

"Thank you, darling. The feather, we place on the handkerchief like so. This is also for the horses, you see. It ensures that their steps are light and also provides ease for them in pulling the carriage. I always add it last because I don't want it to blow away or go cockeyed. It is very important that you align the feather correctly, or else you might make the whole thing unbalanced. Which is, of course, the exact opposite of what you want to do for the horses. We want to make it easier for them, not harder. Now, I think that's properly even. So…" He straightened. "The incantation." He held his hand over the inscription and made a circular motion with his palm over the inscription and the pile on the handkerchief, muttering to himself.

Pip could not explain how he knew the spell had taken hold, but he did.

"There, you see?" the viscount said. "Next is the cleanup." He held out his hand for the bag and placed the letter opener, the compass, the handkerchief, and the feather inside. He pocketed the watch and then he wiped out the inscription with his hand until there was no hint that it had ever been there. He dusted off his hands with a satisfied expression. "Now," he said, guiding Pip back into the coach. "We shall have to repeat the spell in about twenty or so miles, I think. But I believe that will do the trick. Onward, my good man," he said to the driver, climbing into the coach behind Pip.

The coach sped down the road. It was the fastest Pip had ever traveled in his life. He looked out the window to see the countryside whirring past.

"Any questions about the spell, dear?"

Pip was startled by the question. "I've never seen magic done like that before, sir," he said. "I appreciate you showing me."

"You can do it when we stop again. I'll help, of course, and answer all your questions."

"Me?" Pip squawked in alarm. "You want me to—? But, my lord, I can't do magic. I never have before."

"Well, there's always a first time," was the cheery reply. "Not to fret, my sweet, I'll see that it's done properly."

Despite the viscount's assurances, Pip did fret. He fretted for several hours while the coach rocketed through the countryside, wondering frantically when they would reach the twenty-mile mark. Lord Finlington, unaware of Pip's inner turmoil, read a book. When the coach pulled to a stop some time later, he closed the book with a snap and lightly tapped Pip on the knee with it.

"Come along, dear. Let's give it a go, shall we?" He tossed the book on the seat and stepped out of the coach.

Pip followed, with much more trepidation than he had felt the first time. He took the bag that the viscount handed him and, opening it with trembling fingers, he pulled out the feather carefully. The viscount reached forward and took it from him.

"Very good," he said. "You're doing fine, darling. Go on."

Pip pulled out the handkerchief and set it before the horses, careful to see that it lay flat.

"Excellent. You have a mind for details. Always a good sign. See if you can tilt it to lay straight, can you, dear? Sort of align it with the coach and the horses. It's another balancing component, you see."

Pip did as instructed. Then he pulled out the compass and laid it on the handkerchief. The viscount passed him the watch so he could lay it down as well. He pulled out the letter opener, and crouched, feeling at a loss.

Lord Finlington crouched beside him. "Not to worry, dear. It's just a straight line this way," he said, indicating with his finger.

Pip sketched a line into the ground with the blade.

"You poor darling, no need to tremble so! You're doing a marvelous job. Now, draw an arch this way and…" Lord

Finlington continued, detailing the rest of the symbol for Pip, who duly drew it into the road.

"Now," the viscount said, standing and handing him his walking stick. "The next part is simple. Just a circle around the horses and the carriage and the spell here. Don't worry about it being pretty or perfect. You're just laying a boundary, you see."

"Won't it damage your stick, sir?" Pip said, taking it.

The viscount laughed. "You sweet thing, I carry it just for this purpose."

Pip slowly traced a line around the carriage, taking care to bring both ends together. The viscount handed him the feather. Pip placed it on the handkerchief and nudged it until it lay centered between the watch and the compass and parallel to the handkerchief edges.

"Wonderful," the viscount said, clapping his hands. "Quite perfect, darling. You are a natural. I'll teach you the incantation later, of course. But you did a fine job of it."

Pip stepped back while the viscount did the incantation and passed his hand over the spell. When he felt the spell take hold, he let out a breath.

Lord Finlington smiled at him. "That was very good for your first time, Pip. Quite strong, I expect. You really do have talent, darling. You should be very proud of yourself. Now, the cleanup is just as important as the setup. You see, if you don't put away everything, you might leave some residual magic for someone else to pick up along the way. I'm sure most people wouldn't mind a little speed to their travel—but it might not be balanced properly for them, depending on where their coach hits it."

Pip handed the watch back first. The viscount took it in exchange for the bag. Then Pip put everything else back. He wiped out the inscription until he was sure there were no scratches left on the ground.

The viscount peered over Pip's shoulder. "That should do

it. I daresay we will be set all the way to Bedfordshire," he said. "Very good, come along."

"What about the circle, sir?" Pip said before getting inside.

Lord Finlington beamed. "Excellent query, darling. You needn't worry about that. With the sigil gone, the circle is just a circle. It is no longer binding anything."

Pip got inside the coach with the viscount following after. Pip didn't relax until they had traveled for a quarter of an hour with no mishaps.

The viscount chuckled. "I assure you, dear, that I would not have done the incantation unless I was perfectly satisfied with the preparation."

"What kind of shop did you say Miss Hartford has?"

The viscount smiled. "A spell shop. It is another reason I thought you might be a suitable fit. Once Miss Hartford has you trained up a bit in spellcasting, I imagine your assistance will prove invaluable. She will be quite fortunate to have you."

Pip felt himself blush. "You think Miss Hartford will train me, sir?"

"If I know Gerry, I think she will relish the opportunity to train someone. And if she does not, I will."

Pip nodded, his mind whirring. He had not anticipated this aspect of his new life. When he had discovered Nell's propensity for magic, he had hoped she might teach him. At the time, it had seemed like a fun hobby or possibly a useful tool for thievery. But learning magic from an educated lady, a professional, was a prospect he had never imagined for himself.

Of course, when Nell left to be trained by Lord Finlington, she invited Pip to join her. He knew at the time that leaving Jack was not really an option for him. Now he was leaving Jack and London and everything he had ever known behind. He was barreling toward a new place, a new future, and a great many possibilities. Pip had never experienced possibilities and it was a whole new feeling to have them. He sat with the feeling, realizing it frightened him.

The viscount, having sensed that the conversation was over, returned to his book. Pip leaned his head against the side of the coach. He closed his eyes and allowed the rocking motion to lull him to sleep.

"Wake up, darling. We're nearly there." He felt a gentle touch on his knee.

When he opened his eyes, the viscount withdrew his hand. The coach had slowed and Pip could see that dusk had settled. He rubbed his eyes and looked out the window to see open countryside, woods, and fields. It felt like a different world entirely.

"This is it, sir?"

"This is Tutting-on-Cress, yes. Well, really, this is the estate attached to Charlie's house. It is about three miles from the village. I've let a house as well, a couple of miles from here. It really was dreadfully convenient for so much property to be available just when we needed it. When I sent Charlie ahead of us, we agreed to meet at his house for dinner upon our arrival. He will have informed Miss Hartford of the situation. And," he added, "will hopefully have acquired you a new wardrobe. Charlie is brilliant in such matters, you know."

"He bought me clothes?" Pip said, guilt twisting his stomach.

"Not to worry, dear. He has excellent taste and a brilliant eye for size. I'm sure he'll have picked out some splendid things for you. You're much the same size as his Mr. Hartford, in fact. I imagine that will have helped."

Pip did not know what to say. If Mr. Kentworthy had purchased clothes for him, it meant there was yet another person to whom Pip was indebted. First, Lord Finlington for arranging his release, his travel, his job, and his wages. Then, Miss Hartford for taking him on as an employee, regardless of whether or not she really wanted to. If she really did teach him magic, that would add to his debt significantly. And now Mr. Kentworthy had purchased his clothes and seemed prepared to house him for a period of time. He didn't even know how much had been purchased or to what expense. He knew he could never afford the sorts of things Mr. Kentworthy wore, not in his own lifetime. He had to hope that the gentleman had bought things appropriate for Pip's station and new career. He closed his eyes at the realization that he had once again managed to pile up an insurmountable amount of debt.

"All right there, darling?" the viscount said gently, bringing him out of his own reverie.

"Yes," he said, smiling at the gentleman. "Sorry, sir. Just… nervous about meeting Miss Hartford so soon."

Lord Finlington grinned back. "I am sure you will like her. And I am positively certain she will just adore you."

Pip did not share the viscount's confidence, so he said nothing in response.

CHAPTER 3

THE HOUSE WAS SO GRAND, it took Pip's breath away. It was several stories high with columns framing the entryway. Vines and plants climbed up the brown stones of the building. More windows than he cared to count glinted in the fading light. He hovered in the coach door, staring up at the building, his mouth open.

Lord Finlington chuckled as he helped Pip out of the carriage. "Come along, darling. Let's get you fed."

Pip followed obediently.

They were greeted by a liveried butler who led them through the house. Once inside, Pip felt very small indeed. He had never been in such a big building before. The viscount's townhouse felt like it fit within the city. But Mr. Kentworthy's country house was massive, and if Pip hadn't feared making the viscount wait for him, he would have been too awed to move.

The butler escorted them to a large sitting room. The room had three sofas and twice as many chairs, as well as spindly tables covered with decanters, candelabras, and vases. A large painting of a ship filled part of one wall and Pip spotted a sculpture of a man fighting a bull in one corner. In the center of the room, a group of people sat. Pip recognized Mr. Kentworthy, but the other three people were strangers to him.

Mr. Kentworthy saw them first. He smiled and came forward to greet them. "Thank goodness," he said. "Haberforth, tell Jennings to ready the bath, would you please?"

"Pip, dear, you remember Mr. Charles Kentworthy?" Lord Finlington asked.

Mr. Kentworthy was tall and broad shouldered. He was a handsome gentleman with tan colored skin, dark angular eyes, and black hair. He had a wide mouth that tilted upwards in good humor, much like the vicount's. Pip had been quite struck by Mr. Kentworthy's good looks the first time they had met. He would have been intimidated by the gentleman, as Pip had a tendency to be intimidated by tall people, but the man had been of such pleasant disposition as to almost put Pip at ease.

Mr. Kentworthy smiled and bowed. "A pleasure to meet you again."

"And allow me to introduce the Dukex of Molbury, Mr. Gavin Hartford, and Miss Geraldine Hartford. Your Grace, Mr. and Miss Hartford, allow me to present Mr. Philip Standish."

It was, Pip realized, the first time the viscount had addressed him by his full name. He wondered if the formality was due to the mixed company or if it marked a shift in their relationship. He worried a little that it might be the latter and swallowed against the sudden sadness of losing the easy companionship the viscount had shown him all day.

Miss Hartford was a young woman about Pip's age. She was a little taller than he was, though not as tall as Nell. She had prominent cheekbones and a narrow nose. Her hair was a beautiful copper color that softened the severity of her other features. Pip was not attracted to women, but he did recognize that Miss Hartford was likely considered very beautiful. She was also grinning as if she was truly pleased to see him.

"Mr. Standish," she said, coming forward to clasp his hands. "It is wonderful to finally meet you. Nell has told me so much about you. When Charles said that you were coming to work with me, I couldn't believe my luck! We shall have such a capital time!"

Pip realized quite suddenly why Lord Finlington had been so sure of Miss Hartford's positive reaction to the situation. It seemed to Pip that she was the sort of person who found pleasure in everything.

"Don't crowd the poor man, Gerry, for God's sake," Mr. Hartford said.

"Oh, pish tosh, Gavin. He's practically family, after all."

Mr. Hartford rolled his eyes. He looked very much like his sister, with light pink-toned skin, high cheekbones, dark eyes, and narrow nose. He had a beautiful mouth, although unlike Mr. Kentworthy, Lord Finlington, and Miss Hartford, his did not seem as inclined to smile. His wavy dark brown hair glinted red in the candlelight.

"Pleasure to meet you, Mr. Standish," he said courteously. "Please don't mind my sister. She tends to overwhelm people at first meeting. I daresay you'll get accustomed to it."

Miss Hartford did not seem offended by this assessment of her character. She smacked her brother playfully on the shoulder.

The dukex was short, about the same height as the two Hartford siblings (although everyone was taller than Pip), and round. Pip recognized some features in their face that were similar to the viscount—the same full mouth, the same light brown hair, and their eyes held a similarly kind expression.

They smiled down at Pip and said, "You look tired, child. Was it a long trip?"

Pip bit his lip and nodded. He couldn't admit it, but he did feel overwhelmed. Contrary to what Mr. Hartford had said, however, it wasn't Miss Hartford's fault; it was from having a group of such grand people smiling down at him so pleasantly. He bowed to the group, realizing belatedly that he hadn't done so yet, and then looked down shyly. The carpet was very fine, and Pip thought suddenly that his dirty shoes were probably tracking mud and grime all over it. His awareness spread to one of his own apparel and he felt horribly self-conscious all of a sudden. He hunched forward slightly at the thought.

Mr. Kentworthy came to his rescue. "I imagine our Mr. Standish has had a very exciting day. Come along, my dear, let's get you cleaned up and then we'll have dinner." He strode forward and put a light hand to Pip's upper back, guiding him out of the room.

As they left, Pip heard the others asking the viscount about their trip. He wondered if they all knew of his former life as a thief and subsequent imprisonment. The thought that they might speak of it while he was out of the room made him feel small and unworthy.

Mr. Kentworthy walked him upstairs to a room with a large four-poster bed and a window that looked out onto a garden. There was a window seat with a cushion more plush than any mattress Pip had slept on. He wondered vaguely what the bed would be like; he had never actually *slept* in a nice bed before. Mr. Kentworthy walked him to an adjoining room with a tiled floor and a large bath. Two servants were filling the bath with hot water.

"Now," said Mr. Kentworthy. "You must be exhausted, poor thing. Take a bath, take as long as you'd like, and come downstairs when you're ready. I took the liberty of acquiring you some clothes. Don't worry if they don't fit perfectly. We'll see that you're outfitted properly later. I'll have Jennings lay something out for you and he'll help you get dressed." He turned to go and then pivoted back around. "Oh, and I imagine you're hungry. Are you starving, darling? We shall have dinner as soon as you come down.

But if you need a bite now, I can have something brought up for you."

Pip felt a little dazed. "Thank you very much, sir," he said. "I think I can wait until dinner."

"Wonderful," Mr. Kentworthy said, giving him a dazzling smile. "You can change your mind, you know. If you do, just tell Jennings and he'll bring something for you to snack on. All right?"

Pip was soon left with the two servants. One of them, Jennings, Pip supposed, stepped forward and offered to help Pip undress. Feeling horribly embarrassed, Pip shook his head and began undressing himself. Jennings didn't seem perturbed and collected Pip's discarded clothing with a completely neutral expression. Neither he nor the footman made any comment on Pip's nakedness or how wretchedly dirty he was. Jennings passed the bundle of clothes to the other footman, who left the room. Pip stepped nervously up to the bath, and Jennings gently took his arm and helped him into the water.

"Shall I help you bathe, sir?" Jennings asked politely.

Pip shook his head, feeling his face flush.

Again, Jennings did not appear to be offended. He offered Pip a sponge and then stepped away, standing with his back to Pip to provide some privacy.

Slowly, Pip scrubbed at layers of dirt and grime that had accumulated on his skin, and the bathwater quickly became grey and murky. He felt suddenly overwhelmed with the evidence of how poorly he fit into the house, and into the new life he had been given. Feeling a little frantic, he tried scrubbing faster, but the water got murkier and he had barely cleaned the top of his arm. Panic bubbled in his chest, and before he could stop himself, he drew his knees up to his chest, folded himself over them, and started to sob.

He heard Jennings step out of the room and say something in hushed tones to the footman, who was apparently standing outside. Pip knew that he was making a complete fool of himself, but he couldn't stop. He was sitting in a deliciously warm bath in a beautiful house. The people downstairs waiting for him had been nothing but scrupulously kind. He had been promised dinner and a new life full of possibilities. And yet, everything about it felt wrong. He didn't fit. He didn't belong. Even the bathwater was revolting against the notion.

He was startled when Jennings spoke to him, gently, and much nearer than he would have expected. "I'm sure it must all be very new and strange, young sir. Allow me to help."

Pip looked up to see that Jennings had taken off his jacket and rolled up his sleeves. Pip surrendered up the sponge and allowed himself to be bathed by the servant's kind and careful ministrations. It made him feel absolutely wretched to be bathed by someone who most certainly outranked him. He worried that Jennings must realize this too and would despise him for it. But the man never gave any indication of such feelings, only softly telling Pip when to lean forward or lean back, raise an arm or a leg, or bow his head.

At one point, the footman returned, and Jennings paused in bathing Pip to hand him a cup of tea. "It may help," he said.

Pip took the cup and drank. The comforting warmth of the tea made him feel wobbly and weepy all over again. Jennings very kindly did not comment on it. He took the cup away as soon as Pip had emptied it and continued to bathe him.

It took far longer to get clean than Pip would have expected, which heartily embarrassed him. When he finally stepped out of the tub, he was mortified by how dark the water had gotten.

Jennings helped him out and, without asking this time, set about drying Pip down with a soft towel. When he was satisfied that Pip was dry enough, he guided him back to the bedroom. A fire had been built while Pip was bathing and

Jennings led him to stand in front of it before dressing him. As he had been with the bath, Jennings was patient and gentle, softly directing Pip to make the dressing easier. He saved the cravat for last, tying it in a simple knot. He held up a looking glass and Pip felt another wave of emotion crash over him as he stared at his own reflection, looking like a toff and not the worthless thief he knew himself to be.

Jennings swiftly put away the looking glass and handed Pip a handkerchief.

"I'm so sorry, Jennings," Pip said, wiping his eyes.

"Not to worry, sir," Jennings said. "You have nothing to apologize for. Allow me?" he said, taking the handkerchief back. He put it to Pip's nose and told him to blow, which Pip did, even though he felt like a little child and utterly ridiculous.

After Jennings stepped away, Pip sank onto a chair and put his head in his hands. "What you must think of me," he said.

Jennings dismissed the footman. As soon as the door clicked shut, he said, "Might I be so bold as to speak plainly, sir?"

Pip was surprised into looking up. "Of course."

After a brief hesitation, Jennings pulled another chair forward and sat in it. "You will forgive me, I hope, sir, for being so forward. But I do know a little of your situation and what brought you here."

Pip sniffed and Jennings handed him the handkerchief with a doleful smile. Pip blew his nose and waited for the footman to continue.

"You have, if I'm not mistaken, had a very difficult life. I imagine it will take some adjusting to become accustomed to your new life here."

Pip ran a hand through his wet hair. "I'm not even fit to clean your shoes, Jennings. You shouldn't have to be bathing me and serving me. I don't deserve any of it."

Jennings leaned back in his seat. "I have been in service all of my life, sir, and have served several families in my time. I have been Mr. Kentworthy's personal valet for over ten years. He is a very rare sort of gentleman. He appreciates the humanity of a person, even servants." He paused. "Especially servants. I have never served a person for whom I have such respect. If Mr. Kentworthy deems you to be worthy of his help, however he chooses to give it, then I'm inclined to trust his judgment."

Pip had nothing to say to that. Jennings was wrong, of course. But his mind was too jumbled to sort out Jennings's honesty and his own messy feelings.

Jennings leaned forward and gave Pip a very direct look. "If I may offer you some advice, young sir: Be patient with yourself. You've come a long way and you're far from everything you're used to. It will take some time for you to settle. That does not make you ungrateful or foolish and it does not make you undeserving."

Pip closed his eyes and nodded.

There was a soft knock at the door, and it opened before Jennings had a chance to even get up. Mr. Kentworthy stepped into the room and took in the scene with a look of evident concern. "Is everything all right?" he said, closing the door behind him.

Jennings stood, seemingly unembarrassed for having been caught in so informal a conversation with a guest. "I believe, sir, that the young gentleman has had a very…long day."

"Ah," Mr. Kentworthy said with a sigh. "I see. Will you set out a nightshirt, Jennings? Then would you be so kind as to have my guests informed that they should proceed into dinner without me? I won't be a moment. Please have a plate brought up for Mr. Standish, if you would."

Jennings bowed, looking, to Pip's surprise, pleased by the set of instructions. He laid a nightshirt on the bed and then slipped out of the room, closing the door behind him.

Mr. Kentworthy took Jennings's vacated seat. "Do you want to talk about it?" he said gently.

Pip didn't know how to answer the question. He felt wrung out and was not sure if Mr. Kentworthy would understand. Jennings had understood a little, in his way, but Pip felt sure no one would be able to rectify his conflicting emotions. He ran a hand through his wet hair again, trying to come up with a suitable answer. Mr. Kentworthy didn't rush him.

Finally he said, "Would it be all right if I asked you to call me Pip, sir? Mr. Standish feels too...grand for the likes of me. And after everything you've done—"

"I would be glad to call you Pip. But I must ask you not to address me as 'sir.' And if we are on first names, I would be pleased if you called me Charles."

Pip looked at him dubiously. Mr. Kentworthy chuckled. "I'm not one to stand on ceremony, Pip. You are here as a friend. My friends call me Charles."

"I'm sorry you all waited for me for dinner. I'm afraid the bath...it took a bit longer than anticipated."

"It was my mistake, dear. I did not take into account what a trying day this must have been for you. In fact, if I'm not mistaken, I believe this is your first time out of London, yes?"

"Yes, sir."

"Was it a pleasant trip? I believe Bertie got you here in very good time."

"Yes, sir, thank you."

Mr. Kentworthy gave a small smile at the "sir" but did not comment. "Bertie told us that you placed the second speed spell. Very impressive."

Pip looked at him in alarm. "Well, he told me what to do. I've never—that is, it was my first—it wasn't all that impressive, sir. I only placed things where he told me."

"Well, speaking as someone who has no great talent for magic, I will say that speed spells are notoriously fiddly things. I'd never travel with them if I didn't have a driver who was a talented spellcaster. Many people forgo them as a great deal can go wrong."

Pip's mouth went dry. "Really? He didn't say—"

Mr. Kentworthy laughed. "No, he wouldn't. Magic comes easily to Bertie. And he has a better eye for spotting magical talent than anyone I know. He knew what he was doing when he had you perform it, not to worry. Gerry—that is, Miss Hartford—was very pleased to hear about the casting. I believe she's very much looking forward to teaching you herself."

"That's very kind of her."

"Oh, I daresay she'll get as much fun out of the endeavor as you will."

Jennings returned at that juncture. "A tray is being brought up, sir. I thought I might help Mr. Standish change for bed."

"Oh, Lord, Jennings," Pip said, standing. "And after all the work you put into getting me dressed too. I am sorry."

"Nothing to apologize for, young sir. I think the rest will do you good."

"So will the food," Mr. Kentworthy said as he stood. "You look peakish, darling. See that he eats, Jennings, will you?"

"Certainly, sir."

"I'll go back down to my other guests." He laid a hand on Pip's shoulder. "Send for me if you need anything, all right?"

Pip nodded, trying to imagine what he might need Mr. Kentworthy for.

Jennings made quick work of undressing him and helped into a night shirt. Pip then slid into bed, which was every bit as comfortable as he might have hoped. When the dinner tray was brought up, Pip ate in a daze. He started to nod off mid-bite and Jennings gently got him settled on the pillows and whisked the tray away. He was asleep before the valet had left the room.

CHAPTER 4

PIP WAS MUCH ALARMED when he woke the next morning. He panicked for a moment, thinking Jack sent him to bed with a toff and he had forgotten about it. But when he sat up and looked around the room, the preceding day came rushing back to him.

He fell back onto the pillows, feeling weighed down by the memory. He lay still under the covers, reveling in the comfort, and thinking about what Jennings had advised him the night before, to be patient with himself.

He sighed, thinking he would certainly need patience, considering how long it would take him to repay Mr. Kentworthy for the dinner clothes alone. He wasn't much good at sums, but he had a feeling he wouldn't earn enough at the shop to pay anyone back in a hurry, if ever. He hoped Mr. Kentworthy and Lord Finlington would be kinder about it than Jack had been; he didn't think they were the type to hold such things over a person's head. But then, he barely knew them. Jack had seemed kind too, once.

Thinking about his erstwhile lover gave Pip a rush of mixed emotions. It felt strange to wake up in a bed without the other man beside him, and to go so long without Jack's touch. He realized that Jennings was practically the only person who had touched him the previous day, and being bathed and dressed had felt vastly different from Jack's fingers constantly stroking and petting him.

These realizations made Pip feel both free and frightened. It was nice to not be claimed by another person. He didn't think any of the people he met the previous night would feel entitled to his body, a liberating sensation in itself. But the freedom terrified him in a way he could never have predicted. He felt, all at once, very much alone.

The door opened and Jennings came in with a pitcher. He smiled when he saw that Pip was awake. "I came in to lay out your clothes for the day, sir," he said. "I hope you slept comfortably."

"Very," Pip said, sitting up.

Jennings's smile widened. "I'm glad to hear it, sir. Mr. Kentworthy and Mr. and Miss Hartford are having breakfast downstairs, sir. Would you like to join them or would you prefer to have a tray brought up?"

Pip felt his face get hot at the thought of being waited on again while in bed. "I'll go downstairs," he said.

"Very good, sir. I have brought some water. You can freshen up a bit first if you like and then I will help you dress."

Pip climbed out of bed. He splashed water on his face and dried it with the towel. Then he stood in front of another set of fine clothes. He stroked the waistcoat. "How much would you say all this is worth, Jennings?"

The valet laughed. "More than my wages, that's certain."

Pip felt dread thickening at the pit of his stomach.

"Not to worry, young sir," Jennings said. "I'm sure Mr. Kentworthy will keep you well stocked."

"But I can never repay him," Pip said. "Surely he must know that?"

Jennings frowned. "I hardly think he expects you to."

It was like Jack all over again. Only, to be fair, in much finer circumstances.

Jennings pulled the nightshirt over Pip's head. When Pip started to shiver, Jennings led him over to the fire as he had the previous night.

"Didn't you say you were Mr. Kentworthy's personal valet, Jennings?"

"That's right, sir. Over ten years."

"Is helping me taking away from your usual responsibilities?"

Jennings smiled. "I wouldn't worry about it, sir."

"But I do, Jennings," Pip said earnestly. "I'm already an imposition to all those grand people downstairs. I would hate to impose on you, too."

Jennings looked surprised, but did not slow down in the act of dressing Pip. "You are hardly an imposition, young sir. As far as my responsibilities are concerned, Mr. Kentworthy and I are in agreement that it would be best if I assisted you while you are staying here. I helped him dress earlier and he is already down at breakfast. That will likely be the way of it, I think, with me assisting him before coming here to assist you. At least until I can get someone else trained up to take care of you. There are a few footmen who could use more responsibility and experience. They are taking over some of my other duties for the time being. I assure you that I do not regret missing the opportunity to starch and press shirts and cravats," he said with a grin as he draped the cravat over Pip's neck. He began tying it, his fingers nimble with practice. When he was done, he did not offer up the hand mirror as he had done the night before.

He placed a hand on Pip's shoulder. "If I may be honest with you again, sir."

Pip huffed. "I think you can always be honest with me, Jennings. In fact, I think I prefer it."

Jennings smiled and tilted his head in acknowledgement.

"Then allow me to say that I do not think anyone here considers you an imposition. Unless I miss my guess, Mr. Kentworthy and his lordship have sort of taken you under their wings, if you understand me. Adopted you, you might say. I would be very surprised if they expected you to repay them—not because they know you cannot afford it but because they consider their generosity to be gifts. Not everything comes at a cost."

Pip closed his eyes briefly. "If I may be honest back, Jennings."

"I think I'd prefer it," he replied with a wry smile.

"This isn't the first time I have been helped by a great man." Pip looked down at his hands. "I was very...naive then. I'm not now. Kindness and friendship...they come at a price. I've never been given anything without expectation of some kind of return. Life doesn't work that way."

Jennings squeezed his shoulder and Pip met the valet's gaze. "Whatever that other 'great man' did, sir, it was not a help. Nor was it out of kindness or friendship."

He gave Pip's shoulder another squeeze and then led him out of the room, all the way to where the others were eating breakfast. There was a large table taking up the bulk of the room and a smaller table filled with food against one wall. Mr. Kentworthy sat at the head of the table with Mr. Hartford seated at his side. Miss Hartford sat next to her brother. The dukex was seated across from Mr. Hartford, on Mr. Kentworthy's other side. They all looked up and smiled at Pip when he entered the room.

Mr. Kentworthy stood and walked forward. "Good morning, my dear. Did you rest comfortably?"

"Yes, sir. Very."

Mr. Kentworthy tutted as he led Pip to the board where the food had been laid out. "If you persist in addressing me as 'sir' and 'Mr. Kentworthy,' I will revert to calling you Mr. Standish."

Pip smiled, despite his maudlin mood. "Very good, Charles."

"That's better," he replied, patting him on the back. He proceeded to dish a bit of everything onto Pip's plate.

"Good Lord," Mr. Hartford said. "I can't remember the last time I addressed you as 'Mr. Kentworthy.'"

"That's because you have abominable manners, Gavin," Miss Hartford replied. "Mr. Standish cannot be faulted for being more polite."

Charles laughed.

"You sound like John," Mr. Hartford said.

His sister gasped. "What a perfectly horrid thing to say!"

"Who's John?" Pip asked Charles in a low voice, worried there had been some other gentleman in the house that he had forgotten about.

"Our brother," Miss Hartford replied. "And I am nothing like him, thank you very much. He is exceedingly tiresome."

"Did I tell you he wrote to me?" Mr. Hartford added. "Said he'd like to come visit and get to know Charles better. Wanted to bring Veronica—oh, that's my sister-in-law, Mr. Standish—and their horrid little son."

"To be fair," Miss Hartford said. "Their son isn't horrid yet."

"I'm afraid the poor child hasn't got much of a chance, does he? Anyway, I told him it wasn't my house so I couldn't very well invite him."

"You never told me about this," Charles said, guiding Pip over to a chair.

"And for good reason," Mr. Hartford said. "You'd have said yes. And then where would we be?"

"You know I hate to agree with you..." Miss Hartford said.

"Don't be ridiculous," her brother said. "You'd be miserable if they came to visit."

"Don't worry, Pip," Charles said as he took his own seat. "They're always like this. You'll get used to it."

The dukex chuckled. "I confess I rather enjoy the banter." They took a sip of tea. "I feel as if I never left home."

"Is that why you're eating breakfast with us?" Miss Hartford said.

"In part," they replied, grinning at her.

"What was the other part?" Mr. Hartford said.

"They missed me, of course," Charles said.

They scoffed. "Yes, child, that too."

Pip was a little surprised to hear Charles referred to as a child. In his mind, the gentleman was impossibly elegant and mature.

"And I wished to know Mr. Standish better," they continued.

Pip glanced at them in alarm. He was quite nervous of the older person; they seemed so very regal.

Miss Hartford picked up a teapot that had a little handkerchief draped on top of it and poured Pip a cup of tea. He picked it up and took a sip as soon as she was done.

"Good heavens," she said. "Don't you want sugar or milk, Mr. Standish? I don't know that I've ever had tea with nothing in it before."

Pip felt himself blush. He hastily put the cup down and pushed it back toward her. "I'm sorry, miss. I'm not used to having those things in my tea. Am I meant to?"

Miss Hartford's surprised expression changed instantly into one of sympathy, which made Pip feel even worse. "Not at all, Mr. Standish. You are meant to take tea exactly as you like it. Please forgive me for commenting on it."

Pip wished he could disappear into the floor. They were all looking at him with careful smiles. Well, Miss Hartford, Charles, and the dukex were looking at him with careful smiles; Mr. Hartford was frowning at the teapot. Finally, Mr. Hartford heaved a sigh, picked up the teapot, and poured some into his sister's cup.

"There," he said. "Try it. Plenty of people take their tea

black, Gerry. It isn't all that extraordinary. No offense, of course, Mr. Standish," he added.

"Really, Gavin," Miss Hartford said. "Such manners. You told me you wanted me to pour out while I lived here. So you aren't supposed to pour for me, you realize?" But she picked up her teacup anyway.

Far from being offended, Pip was greatly relieved that the gentleman had shifted the focus so effectively. He began to eat his breakfast while everyone else enjoyed the spectacle of Miss Hartford trying plain tea.

"It is more bitter than I like," she pronounced after a few sips. "But you get a better sense of the actual flavor."

"Good," Mr. Hartford said. "I'm glad that's settled. Are you going to the shop today?"

Miss Hartford rolled her eyes. "I work there, you dolt. Of course I'm going. And Mr. Standish, you are welcome to come and take a look at it, if you'd like."

"Unless you're too tired, my dear," Charles put in. "There is no rush."

Pip shook his head. "No, I'd be pleased to see it. I expected I'd be working today. I'm not too tired," he added to Charles, who beamed at him in response.

Miss Hartford looked pleased. "Lovely! Then we can go as soon as we are done with our breakfasts. It is a pleasant walk," she added. "Barely three miles. I usually walk it, but we can take the carriage if you would prefer."

Pip said, stutteringly, that he would be glad to walk.

She grinned at him. "That's settled then." She took another sip of her tea and gave a small grimace. "Right," she said. "I've tried it." Then she poured a generous splash of milk into her cup and stirred. "What will you two do today?" she asked, turning to Charles.

"Well," Charles said, smiling fondly at Mr. Hartford. "I was thinking it might be a nice morning for a ride. Don't you agree, darling?"

Mr. Hartford nodded solemnly. "I daresay I might enjoy that."

Miss Hartford smiled into her teacup as if she was trying not to laugh. Mr. Hartford frowned a little and glanced at the dukex. "Would that be all right, do you think?"

Charles gave a small sigh.

The dukex smiled fondly at Mr. Hartford. "Yes, poppet. It will be perfectly right. The country is less exacting than town. But I would advise you to return within a couple of hours."

"Thank you, Your Grace."

"And when you return, I'll see to it you know how to pour tea."

Mr. Hartford paled a little. "Must I?"

"You might as well get accustomed to it now, child. You will be taking on the responsibility of hosting when you are married."

Mr. Hartford sipped his tea, but it seemed more like a nervous gesture than anything else.

"You poured for me when I visited your townhouse," Charles said.

"Yes, but it didn't seem to matter if I did it correctly, really." Mr. Hartford glanced at the dukex. "I'm tolerably certain you will want me to do it properly."

"I will," they said with a smile. "Don't fret about it. I'll ease you into things."

Mr. Hartford relaxed a little. "Oh. Like the dancing lessons?"

"Exactly, just like the dancing lessons. We'll start with a short lesson today."

"Thank you, Your Grace."

"If you get bored after that, you might visit us at the shop," Miss Hartford said.

"And get bullied into helping you again?" Mr. Hartford said. "Not a chance of it."

Miss Hartford tutted in mock offense.

Charles laid his hand over Mr. Hartford's and said to Miss Hartford, "We would be delighted to come visit you, Gerry."

"Thank you, Charles," she said pointedly. "Besides, Gavin, Mr. Standish is here to help me now. So you shan't need to do a thing."

"Dashed civil of him, if you ask me," Mr. Hartford said.

Charles chuckled and lifted Mr. Hartford's hand to kiss the inside of his wrist.

Mr. Hartford gave Charles a look of pure adoration before blushing profusely and yanking his hand away. "For God's sake, Charles," he said in a loud whisper. "We have company."

"Oh, Gavin, we are at home," Miss Hartford said. "And I don't think Mr. Standish minds, do you, Mr. Standish?"

Pip shook his head.

"Julian minds," Charles said. "Don't you, darling?"

The dukex raised an eyebrow. "So long as you don't get carried away, Charles, and keep the affection to our small circle—that is, avoid it in more mixed company—I will allow it."

"Very gracious," Charles muttered.

"You see?" Miss Hartford said primly to her brother. "We're all family, or nearly family. I think it's wonderfully romantic, personally."

"Weren't you in such a rage to have me behave properly a few minutes ago?" Mr. Hartford retorted.

"Would you like more food, Pip?" Charles asked, noticing that Pip's plate was almost empty.

"Or tea?" Miss Hartford said. "I promise I won't pester you about your tastes this time."

Pip, feeling fuller than he thought possible, blushed and shook his head. "No, thank you, Miss Hartford, Mr.—I mean, Charles."

"Well, then," Miss Hartford said, draining her own cup of tea. "Would you like to see the shop?"

Pip stood. "Certainly, miss."

She smiled as she took his arm and walked him out of the breakfast room and to the front door. "Oh, do call me Gerry, Mr. Standish. All of my friends do. And I have a feeling we shall become very good friends."

"Are you sure it's all right, miss?" Pip said. "You are my employer, after all."

Her forehead creased slightly. "Good heavens, I do suppose I am." She laughed. "Isn't it funny to think of me being an employer to anyone?"

Pip was saved from having to answer this question by a couple of footmen who approached, their arms full of outer-wear. He was helped into a walking jacket that was startlingly heavy. Then he was handed a pair of gloves, which felt strange to wear, a hat, which made him feel silly and felt far too precarious perched on his head, and a walking stick. The walking stick was nothing so fancy as the one Lord Finlington had sported, but Pip had stolen enough fine things in his life to know he was holding a quality piece.

Miss Hartford, now wearing a spencer jacket and a bonnet, took his arm again and led the way out the door. Pip kept touching the hat to make sure it was still in place.

Before they had walked fifty paces from the house, she stopped, smiled at him and said, "May I?" before gently tugging his hat more firmly on his head.

"Thank you, miss," he said softly.

She tucked her hand around his arm again and led them forward. "Is it true Bertie taught you a speed spell on the way here?"

He nodded.

"How capital!" she exclaimed. "He said you did a wonderful job."

Pip tugged at his collar, self-conscious. "I'm not sure I'd go so far as to say that, miss."

"Oh, do call me Gerry," she said. "You know I was only

teasing Gavin about being proper, don't you? I'm not really so very stuffy."

Pip gave a small smile. "I don't think I'd ever describe you as stuffy, Miss Hartford."

"Thank goodness," she said. "I suppose we'll have to work up to Gerry, won't we?"

"I'm sorry, Miss…Miss Hartford. It doesn't feel right. It doesn't feel right addressing Mr. Kentworthy by his given name either."

"How did he persuade you to do it?"

"He agreed to call me Pip."

She seemed to consider this. "Would it help if I called you Pip? I don't mean to presume, of course."

"No, Miss Hartford, not at all. I much prefer Pip. Mr. Standish feels far too grand for me."

"As does Miss Hartford. Do you see my problem?" she persisted.

"If you don't mind my saying, miss, it isn't my place to call people like you and Mr. Kentworthy by their given names."

She stopped and turned to him. "Perhaps it wasn't a week ago," she said, looking serious. "Actually," she added, frowning to herself, "I take that back. A week ago, you were still Nell's best friend. I consider Nell *my* friend. So if I had met you last week, I still would have asked you to call me by my name, even if we weren't working together. Nell didn't seem to mind calling me Gerry."

He puffed out his cheeks. "Nell's different."

She tilted her head. "How so?"

He shrugged, which felt more constricted in all of the layers he was now wearing. "She's always been…meant for great things."

He had believed for a long time that Nell's destiny lay beyond the dingy alleyways in which they'd grown up. He knew she believed it, too. It showed in the tilt of her chin, in the boldness with which she held herself, in the forthright way she spoke, and in the way she was unafraid to pursue what she felt she deserved. He had long been awed by Nell's ambition, her certainty that she deserved better. She had always approached life with a courage he could not begin to obtain. He was sure she wouldn't have been as cowed as he was by his current circumstances. The thought made him feel even worse.

"And you haven't?" Miss Hartford asked gently.

He shook his head. "No, miss. I haven't any of Nell's grand ambitions. I've always known where I belong. I've never had any illusions as to my worth."

"Your *worth*?" she said.

"You know I was a thief," he said.

"So was Nell."

"Yes, but she chose not to be. Twice."

"Your circumstances were different than hers. You had other reasons keeping you there."

He looked at the ground, focusing on the way the dirt moved when the walking stick struck it. "She told you then?"

"Well, she does talk about you a great deal."

He winced. "Oh."

A small gloved hand settled on his chest. "You have nothing to be ashamed of, Pip."

Pip gave a humorless laugh and looked away, frustrated by the tears that were threatening to fall. He gripped his walking stick, suddenly glad he had something to hold. He sniffed, annoyed that Miss Hartford should be the second person to see him cry since arriving at the house—the third, when he remembered the footman in his bedroom the night before. A handkerchief fluttered in his peripheral vision and he accepted it, grateful and embarrassed.

At the sound of hooves behind them, Pip closed his eyes and groaned inwardly. He quickly tucked the handkerchief into his fist and turned away from the noise.

"Everything all right?" he heard Charles say.

"Oh, yes," Miss Hartford said blithely. "I was just realizing that I'm not at all sure Pip's shoes will be comfortable for walking all the way to town. It would not do for him to form blisters before he's even started work."

"You're quite right, Gerry," Charles said, matching her tone. "I didn't even think of walking boots. Silly of me, I now realize. We'll get some today when we're in the village. I'll ride back to the house and have them ready the carriage for you, shall I?"

"Thank you, Charles," Miss Hartford said.

Out of the corner of his eye, he saw her make a shooing motion and heard the other horse canter away after the first. He sighed. "Thank you, Miss Hartford."

"Don't mention it, Pip," she replied. Gently, she took his arm again and started walking them back towards the house. "I hope you know," she said after a few moments, "that you are among friends now."

He swallowed, his throat feeling tight. "I'm afraid that is also a somewhat new experience for me."

She squeezed his arm.

"Curses," he said, stopping and unfolding the hand-kerchief.

She politely looked away while he dabbed at his eyes.

"I'm sorry to have deprived you of your walk."

She laughed. "I wasn't lying, you know. Those shoes are not meant for long walks. They were purchased, I imagine, for standing around in a shop all day. Don't worry. We have plenty of long walks ahead of us, I think."

Pip nodded and they trudged back to the house. Mr. Kentworthy and Mr. Hartford saw them into the carriage which then trundled down the road into Tutting-on-Cress. Miss Hartford very kindly did not say another word about his tears, his worth, his past, or his shame.

CHAPTER 5

TUTTING-ON-CRESS was a small village in the countryside, so Pip was surprised by how many people bustled about. It occurred to him that they ought to have arrived early in the morning to open the shop, but he knew the delay had been his fault, so he said nothing. He stepped out of the carriage and tentatively helped Miss Hartford out. She gave him a huge smile and a small wink, then walked briskly to a little shop. She pulled a key out of her reticule and opened the door.

Pip never had occasion to enter a spell shop, so he had no grounds for comparison, but he was a little amazed at how clean and tidy the small shop was. There was a wide window at the front of the store, with a long counter placed a little ways in front of it. The walls on either side were lined with long hooks. On each hook hung a row of drawstring bags, much like the one Lord Finlington had kept in his pocket. Black slates with chalked words hung above each section of bags. Pip supposed those explained what was in each bag. He had never learned to read, and up until that moment, it had never occurred to him that it might be a drawback in this new profession. He wondered how long he'd be able to keep such a thing from Miss Hartford. He didn't want to sink any lower in her estimation than he likely already had.

He walked slowly through the store, eyeing the nearly identical bags and wishing he could pick them up and peek inside. He had a feeling that this would not be an appropriate thing to do, so he gripped his walking stick with one hand and turned away from the bags to look at the rest of the shop. The wall on the far end was lined with shelves. These were covered with jars, bottles, boxes, and tools. They were all labeled as well, which made Pip feel even more anxious. Perhaps he would not have to spend much time at the front of the shop.

There was a doorway on one side of the far wall in which a curtain was hanging. Miss Hartford strolled past him and pushed the curtain open. "We can put our things in here," she said over her shoulder.

He followed her to the back room, took off his hat and gloves, and placed them next to hers. He hung his cloak on a small peg on the wall next to her jacket and, after a moment of indecision, leaned the walking stick against the wall beneath his cloak.

Miss Hartford then walked him around the back room, pointing to where she kept the ingredients, where she put the spells together, and where she experimented with new ones. She explained all of the tools and how she used them. She showed him a little closet where she stored a broom, a dustpan, a duster, a mop, a bucket, and a great many washcloths. "Magic is a messy business," she said.

She opened a door at the back of the workroom that revealed a narrow staircase and explained that it led to a small flat above the shop where the previous owner used to live.Then she showed him where she kept her work aprons and the gloves she used for spell building. She handed him one of the aprons and helped him tie it on, then put one on herself and turned so he might return the favor. It felt intimate and Pip was not at all sure that it was appropriate for him to help a lady like Miss Hartford with her apron, but she clearly had no such reservations.

"I haven't been running the shop for very long," she admitted, walking back out to the front. "Mr. Fenshaw left it to me a couple of months ago. He helped me to run it for about a month until he felt confident I could handle things, so I'm not even sure what you ought to do." She put her hands on her hips and looked around the store, as if hoping for inspiration to strike. Then, she gave him a careful look. "Can you read, Pip?"

Pip felt his face get hot. He shook his head.

Miss Hartford didn't seem surprised. "I thought not. Nell couldn't read either until Bertie started to teach her. We shall carve out time for reading lessons then."

"That's very kind of you, miss," he said, embarrassed. "But I do hate to be an imposition."

"Nonsense," she said. "It would be a great deal of help to me if you can read. Not that I'm suggesting purely for my own benefit, of course. But you would be better able to assist customers if you can read the labels and help me write them. I'm often making new spells, you see," she went on. "It's one of the reasons Mr. Fenshaw left me the business. He said I represented a new generation of spellmasters." She grinned, clearly proud of this. "So, the inventory will be constantly changing as I experiment and find out what people need and like. Besides, we will be setting up time for you to learn magic, so adding reading to the curriculum will be no trouble."

"I'm sorry, Miss Hartford. I do so want to be useful to you. I'm afraid I'm not as well prepared for this work as I would have liked."

She patted him on the shoulder. "Not to worry. I feel better about this business already, having you here. It's nice to have someone to muddle along with me." She smiled. "I'm afraid I'm not as well prepared for this work as I would have liked either. So, we shall have to learn together."

He smiled. "Very good," he said. He considered a moment, looking at her in her work apron. She was still very clearly a lady, with the way she held herself and the way she talked. But here in the shop, both of them wearing aprons over their fine clothes, it seemed different somehow. He was still nothing like her equal, but given her own confession about being new to her line of work, he felt on firmer ground at last.

"I think," he said shyly, "that I might call you Gerry while we are at the shop."

She beamed and clapped her hands together. "Capital!"

In the end, Gerry settled on having Pip observe her in the shop for the day. She flipped the sign on the door so that everyone would know they were open. Between customers, she would explain what each spell was and what exactly it did. Pip repeated each one back to her, diligently working to memorize them, hoping to keep his lack of education from being a burden. He watched as she sold to customers, fascinated with her obvious passion for her work. It didn't take long for him to understand why the previous owner had left her the shop. Gerry had a love of magic and clearly wanted to share that with others. She asked every customer if they had ever worked the spell they were purchasing. Whenever a customer said that they hadn't, she would offer to explain it to them. Then she would walk them over to the counter, take each item out, show how to arrange everything, and provide any advice particular to the spell. She was very patient and answered every question as if it was an excellent one.

By the time Charles and Mr. Hartford arrived to visit and escort them home for lunch, Pip was fully in awe of his new employer.

"I'm sure it is a very bad business practice to leave for lunch," she told him with a self-deprecating smile as she locked the door. "But I've decided that if the village is so accepting of a person of my station learning spell building and running a shop, then they will surely be just as accepting of that person running the shop in whatever way she pleases."

"I rather think they already do, Miss Hartford," he said, climbing after her into the carriage.

"Oh dear," she said with a sigh. "We're back to that now, aren't we? Is it the apron?"

He smiled and looked out the window, avoiding the question.

They ate lunch together and then took the carriage back to the village. Charles had presented Pip with a pair of walking boots, but Miss Hartford chose the carriage over the walk in order to return to her shop more quickly. The rest of the day passed smoothly. Pip continued to follow Gerry around the store, watching her with customers. She closed the shop early and then demonstrated how she built spells and restocked the store. He swept and mopped the floor while she put spells together to replace what had been bought. Then she showed him how to help clean up her work space.

By the end of the day, Pip had a small blister under his thumb from holding the broom and mop handles too tightly and he felt more satisfied from his one day of work than he ever had in his life. He even felt better than he had when he and Nell worked together in the street. Those had always been the best days, for he and Nell made a good team, and Pip knew himself to be good at what he did.

But working with Gerry in the shop was so wholly different from anything he had experienced. He had felt nervous and uncomfortable throughout the day, with so much to learn and so much he didn't know. But he never once had to look over his shoulder out of fear. The customers who came in did not look at him with disdain or disgust or even with predatory interest. They seemed to assume that any well-dressed young man working with Miss Hartford must be a gentleman and, as such, he was worthy of respect. People smiled and curtsied or bowed when they met him, which made him feel strange. As he grew a little more comfortable and started to smile back, he found that he was met with blushes and shyness.

In a way, it embarrassed him to be treated with such respect for he was sure that if people knew what he really was and what sort of life he had come from, they would not have been so polite. But it felt almost as though he were playing a part. Just as Miss Hartford became Gerry when she wore an apron over her lovely dress, Pip became a respectable young man in his own apron. It was all a sham, of course. But he told himself that as long as he wore his shop apron, he could play the part that was given to him.

They were just taking off their aprons and putting on their coats when a knock came at the shop door. Gerry went to answer it and returned to the work room with Lord Finlington in tow.

"Darling, how fine you look," the viscount said by way of a greeting. "Charlie really does have an eye for clothes, doesn't he?"

"Thank you, sir," Pip said, feeling self-conscious. He put on his hat, which Miss Hartford adjusted, grabbed his walking stick, and followed the other two out the door.

"As I'm dining with you again tonight, I thought it would be nice to escort you home," the viscount explained as he helped Miss Hartford and then Pip into the carriage.

Miss Hartford took the forward-facing seat and Pip immediately took the seat opposite. He was surprised when Lord Finlington sat next to him. He felt a little shy, sharing a seat with the viscount. The carriage was roomy, but they jostled against each other when the carriage hit bumps on the road and he was disconcerted by Lord Finlington's thigh or arm brushing against his own.

He looked out the window, thinking about how the viscount had said he was taking them home. Pip had never had a home that felt like it was his own. Throughout most of his life, Jack had supplied him with shelter, first by providing Pip with a pallet in a communal area full of other people, and then by sharing his own bed. Now Pip was heading to this new home, full of people he barely knew. Would he ever belong or would he forever feel like an outsider, living off the generosity of others? He was struck with an overwhelming sense of loneliness. He closed his eyes and took a deep breath, willing himself not to cry.

"How was your first day, m'dear?" Lord Finlington said, breaking into his dreary thoughts.

Grateful for the distraction, Pip turned and started to tell him, describing how tidy and organized everything was, how good Miss Hartford was with her customers, and how he had helped to clean up afterwards. Given the fact that Lord Finlington was the reason he had this job, it felt good to be able to give a report, to prove how much he was endeavoring to be worthy. The viscount listened politely, asking questions and giving commentary. Miss Hartford seemed very gratified by Pip's description of her shop and her work style.

"I'm so glad you've come," she said, beaming at him. "It's been lovely having someone else to work with. And when you're all trained up, it will be even better."

Pip gave her a small smile in return, wishing he was better suited to assist her. It was terribly isolating, thinking about how trapped he had felt in his old life and how now, even with a fresh start, he was still trapped by his own past and shortcomings. He gripped his walking stick and found surprising comfort in feeling the blister on his thumb. Idly, he rubbed it against the brass of the walking stick, reveling privately in the proof of his own work.

At length, they reached the house and Pip was treated to a sumptuous dinner. He answered more questions about how his day had gone and was pleased with himself when he thought to ask Charles and Mr. Hartford about their ride. He sipped his wine, rubbing his thumb against the glass or the tablecloth every time he needed a reminder that he had done something well that day. He didn't think anyone had noticed until the party moved from the dining room to the sitting room and Lord Finlington stopped him with a gentle hand on his arm. The dukex glanced over their shoulder at the viscount's hand on Pip's arm and then left, leaving the room empty except for the two of them.

"Is your thumb bothering you, m'dear?" he said.

"Oh," Pip said, feeling himself blush. He curled his hand into a fist and shoved it behind his back. "No, sir. I'm sorry. I didn't think anyone had noticed, sir."

"I'm afraid you'll only aggravate the blister if you keep rubbing at it. I can whip up a little tincture for you. Won't take a moment."

"No, thank you, sir. I—" He hesitated, trying to think of what to say that the viscount might understand. He did not want to go into all his jumbled thoughts. Far too many people knew of his concerns as it was; he dreaded the thought of Lord Finlington becoming one of them. "I suppose it is silly," he said at last. "But helping Miss Hartford clean up the shop was the first thing I did to really help her all day. I like having something to remind me of that."

The viscount smiled. "I understand, darling. Not silly at all." He paused, considering. "It occurs to me, m'dear, that this has been another long day for you. Would you like to retire early?"

"I should hate to be rude—"

"I assure you, no one will think of you as rude."

"But I went to bed early last night," he protested.

The viscount chuckled. "You're allowed to have multiple long days, m'dear. It is quite understandable under the circumstances."

Pip was, in fact, very tired, and very tempted to take the viscount's advice. He was still deciding what to do when Charles came back in.

"Everything all right?" he said.

Pip realized suddenly that Charles often greeted him with that particular question.

"I was just trying to persuade our friend here to retire early," Lord Finlington said.

"Good heavens, of course," Charles said. "You do look tired, dear, if you don't mind my saying so. Why don't we go upstairs? I'll find Jennings for you."

"The others will understand, darling," the viscount assured him.

"Shall I get something for that blister?" Charles said as they walked out of the room.

"No, dear," the viscount said, laughing, from behind them. "I already asked."

Charles walked him back to his room. Pip was barely alone long enough to take his coat off when Jennings came in.

"I made it through dinner this time, Jennings," Pip said. "I daresay that's an improvement, in a way."

"It certainly is, sir," Jennings said with a laugh. He took the coat and hung it up. "Very well done." He helped Pip undress and got him into bed.

And Pip didn't even cry again until the door clicked shut behind the valet. Which was also an improvement, in a way.

CHAPTER 6

AT BREAKFAST THE NEXT MORNING, Pip noticed that Charles, Mr. Hartford, and the dukex were all dressed in more formal clothes. Mr. Hartford poured the tea instead of Miss Hartford, his hands shaking slightly. The dukex soothingly assured him that he had done very well. The young gentleman seemed relieved that Pip's tea took so little work, and Pip was pleased with the knowledge that in tea, at least, he was of little burden to his new friends.

When he and Miss Hartford stood up to go, the other three stood as well. Charles noticed Pip's surprised expression and said, "We're off to church this morning. The dukex insisted."

"It is an excellent way to meet neighbors," the dukex said, following them to the door.

Pip was unsettled with the bustle of everyone putting on their outerwear at once, making the foyer crowded.

The dukex tweaked Mr. Hartford's cravat and brushed the young man's shoulders in a doting way. "You already know some of the people," they said softly. "So it will be even easier than London. You can introduce me to your relations and any other friends you have here and then we'll meet the vicar. All right?"

Mr. Hartford nodded, looking pale. He adjusted his cuffs.

Charles leaned down to kiss his fiancé on the cheek and take his hand. Then he led the way out the door. The carriage was waiting outside for them and Charles helped Mr. Hartford into the carriage first, and then the dukex, before climbing in after. "Have a lovely day at the shop, darlings!" he said cheerily before the carriage moved down the road.

Their day in the shop passed much like the first had. With his new walking boots, Pip was able to walk with Miss Hartford into town. It was a unique experience, walking across the countryside for miles—so different than walking in the city had been. Once at the shop, they were able to open up immediately, now that Pip had already had his tour. He started fetching spells off the hooks for customers, trying to solidify what he remembered from the previous day. Gerry seemed delighted with this practice. The carriage arrived to take them home for lunch. After lunch, they took the carriage back, and then walked home again at the end of the day.

Lord Finlington did not come over every night for dinner. This meant that after dinner, Miss Hartford would sit down with Pip in the library and spend some time on his letters and basic magical theory. Pip did not enjoy the lessons nearly as much as he thought he should. It made him feel embarrassed and uncomfortable to learn things as an adult that other people learned as children. Although he was learning the letters easily enough, practicing the writing was tedious and he was often overwhelmed, sitting in the library, surrounded by volumes that he could not read or understand.

The magical theory was complicated and confusing. Miss Hartford was patient, despite having to repeat her explanations when Pip remained baffled by them. She started with Sandellini's List of Constitutional Properties.

"It is usually encouraged that a person memorize the list," she said. "But I think we can skip that exercise for now."

Pip nearly fainted in relief at that.

She proceeded to explain that an item's Constitutional Properties indicated how it might impact a spell. "For instance, a feather is often what is used to make something float. We use wool or other kinds of fabric to soften things. There are herbs that can be used to make things hot. Does that make sense?"

Pip didn't think it did. The mention of the feather reminded him of the travel spell Lord Finlington had shown him, but he was quite sure the feather hadn't been used to make anything float. Only he couldn't remember *what* the feather had been used for and he felt foolish for forgetting the only spell he'd learned. He was too self-conscious to ask Miss Hartford about it, so instead of voicing his confusion, he nodded.

The next magical lesson was just as confusing. She taught him about Norton's Theorem of Magical Absorbance, but he was so intimidated by the string of long words that he barely heard a thing she said about it. He vaguely understood that the theorem argued that everything could be impacted by magic. But he felt that couldn't be right. He'd seen Nell cast multiple spells that hadn't worked; if everything could be impacted by magic, why hadn't the spells been effective? Then again, asking this question would have meant explaining that Nell had used her magic to break into Lord Finlington's townhouse, and Pip was not at all sure if Miss Hartford knew about that. Deciding it was probably a foolish question anyhow, he didn't ask.

The following day, Miss Hartford told him as they walked home from the shop that she had invited Lord Finlington to visit for dinner.

Pip was always pleased to see the gentleman, so he responded accordingly. However, Miss Hartford went on to explain that she'd hoped the viscount would give her some advice on their magic lessons. "You see, I feel that I am over-whelming you with so much to learn all at once. Reading, writing, and magic, not to mention training in working at the shop. Is it…is it too much?"

He hated the way her forehead creased in concern. He shook his head. "I want to learn all of those things. I was brought here to help you and learning everything will help, won't it?"

"You're already a help to me," she said, patting his arm. "Bertie taught Nell, so I thought he might have some advice on which subjects would be best to wait on. I would say magic, except that you work in a spell shop, so that seems like a silly thing to not teach you. Then again, learning magic will be much easier when you know how to read and write. And—"

"Please," he started, then winced when he realized he had interrupted her. "Please don't change anything on my account. Is it…is it because I'm learning too slowly?" he added quietly.

"Not at all!" she said. "Quite the contrary. You are doing very well. I just…I just think we might be overdoing it a bit. But perhaps Bertie will have some advice on the matter."

When they arrived at home, Miss Hartford pulled Pip and Lord Finlington into a sitting room and explained her concerns to the viscount.

"I've been trying to model my lessons on how you taught Nell," she said. "But I wasn't really there, just visiting, so I'm guessing a great deal."

Lord Finlington considered for a long moment. "Well, I had Nell focus on reading and writing for a full month before we began magic lessons. But, as you pointed out, you both work in a spell shop, so arguments could be made either way. And of course no one's learning styles are quite the same. So even though I taught Nell in one manner, it doesn't neces-sarily follow that Pip needs to learn in the same order." He turned to Pip. "What would be most comfortable for you, m'dear?"

Pip shifted in his seat, embarrassed by the topic. "I want to be helpful to Miss Hartford. I just wish I could learn everything more quickly."

Both Lord Finlington and Miss Hartford opened their mouths to respond, but the door to the sitting room opened and Charles stuck his head in the room. "So sorry to interrupt," he said with a smile that made him look shockingly unapologetic. "Gerry, could I steal you away for a moment?"

She gave Pip's hand a squeeze and followed Charles out of the room.

Lord Finlington turned to him. "I hope you know, m'dear," he said in a quiet voice, "that there is no shame in needing a change to the lessons. As Gerry pointed out, you are learning a great deal all at once."

"You've all done so much for me," Pip said. "The least I can do is learn everything you wish to teach me."

"We are helping you because we wish to. As your friend, I want to see you happy. If making some small adjustments to what you're learning will make you a little happier, we would gladly do it."

Pip felt a small thrill at the reminder of the viscount's friendship. He thought through his words carefully and said, "I'd like to go on learning reading and writing as we have done. I wish I'd learned it a long time ago."

"Of course, m'dear. Should we give you some time before teaching you magic?"

He wanted to admit that magical theory seemed beyond his comprehension, but he was too embarrassed to do so. "I don't know," he said at last. "I've wanted to learn magic since I saw Nell doing it. But...it's very different than what I expected."

Lord Finlington gave a small smile. "Well, to be perfectly honest, my sweet, Nell had to unlearn a great deal of what she'd taught herself. So it's no surprise that what you saw her doing is different than what you're learning now."

"Oh."

"This is really about what you want," the viscount said. "What would make you happy, darling?"

Pip gave the question serious thought. What would make him happy was to have Lord Finlington look at him with wonder, or to admire him, or to tell him how clever he was. He was sure that was unlikely to ever happen if the lessons were changed, so he took a deep breath and said, "I think I'd like to go on learning everything as I have done."

The viscount gave him a long look and said, "Of course, m'dear. And if you change your mind, you know you have only to say the word."

"Thank you."

When Miss Hartford returned to the room, Lord Finlington explained what Pip had decided and they all went in to dinner.

FOR SEVERAL DAYS, HE FELL INTO A FAMILIAR ROUTINE: HE WOULD eat breakfast with the rest of the household, walk to the shop, work until lunch, return home for lunch, work until dinner, and then after dinner he would continue lessons.

With the routine, unfortunately, came restless nights. When he was no longer so tired as to sleep like the dead until morning, Pip would toss and turn, his sheets rumpling around him. Then the nightmares came. Pip dreamt of Jack, of men he'd been sent to bed with, of unwelcome touches. He'd wake up, covered in sweat, and then lie awake until morning.

Being sleep-deprived did not help. But he was determined not to be a burden, so even after Miss Hartford would leave the library, he would remain bent over the writing table, practicing. He would practice until he could barely hold his head up. During these evening practices, everyone in the house seemed to leave him alone, so only one person ever appeared to notice his habit of staying up too late: the Dukex of Molbury. They would walk in every time Pip practiced late into the night and gently pry him away from the writing desk with a soft, "Time for you to go to bed now, child." Then they would walk Pip up to his room and bid him good night.

One evening, Pip was surprised to be visited by Mr. Hartford. He seemed surprised to see Pip in the library, although not displeased. Pip didn't know what to make of the young gentleman. He was older than Pip and Miss Hartford, but Miss Hartford often treated her brother like he was the younger sibling. He was so solemn as to appear gruff at times. Pip was fairly certain the man did not dislike him, but Mr. Hartford seemed accustomed to having his solemnity greeted with teasing, from Charles or Miss Hartford, and even Lord Finlington. Pip did not feel the least bit comfortable teasing the gentleman, so he generally stayed out of his way.

"Ah," he said. "Mr. Standish, good evening. It's nice to know there is someone else in this house who likes to take refuge in the library."

"I am not in your way, am I, Mr. Hartford?"

Mr. Hartford shook his head and began perusing the shelves, pulling books down, seemingly at random. He glanced down to see Pip watching him and then seemed to notice the paper filled with poorly written letters.

Using a book, he gestured toward the paper. "How is it coming along?"

Pip shifted his arm to try to cover up some of the paper. "Well enough, I think," he said. "I wish I were a quicker study."

Mr. Hartford opened his mouth as if to say something, then seemed to think better of it. He abruptly headed for the door and paused, with one hand on the handle. "You will forgive me, I hope, Mr. Standish," he said slowly. "I am not very open by nature. But I think you should know that I admire your courage in coming here."

Pip frowned. "Mr. Hartford, you are aware of the circumstances in my move here, yes?"

"I was with Gerry when Charles explained everything."

"Then, I don't—"

"Just because you did not have very many choices, does not make you any less brave," the gentleman said quietly. "I —" He hesitated and then set his books down carefully on the floor before pulling a chair up to one side of Pip's desk. "Last autumn, my parents sent me to live alone in London for a short time. I could never admit it to anyone then, but I was wretchedly lonely. I knew no one, you see. And it wasn't until Charles—" He paused and a brief, small smile crossed his lips at the memory. "Charles and I met, and he sort of forced me to actually leave the house."

He swallowed. "I do not mean to presume that your circumstances and mine are anything alike. I only wish to say that I understand what it is to be lonely, even when you are surrounded by a great many people. And sometimes…sometimes when you are surrounded by people who make friends easily, it is even more challenging, for they do not understand loneliness so readily."

Pip studied the young man in front of him, struck by the revelation that someone did understand some aspects to his unhappiness.

"Mr. Standish, I know how it feels to be moved suddenly to a new place and to struggle to…fit. And having to learn things so different from what you've always known…it cannot be easy. When I went to London, Charles pushed me into all sorts of new experiences. I thought it such a hardship at the time and all he did was encourage me to go out riding with him and meet new people and take up boxing. It was nothing compared to the education you are receiving."

Pip had no response for this. He rolled the pen in his hand and tried to come up with something to say.

Mr. Hartford continued, "I say all of this to tell you that I understand how lonely it can be and how frightening, strange, uncomfortable, and damned exhausting it can be— how *you* must be. If you ever wish to talk—well, I know you're a fairly private person. At least, I think you are. But if you ever wish to talk about it, I hope you know you can talk to me. Gerry and Charles are the best of people, but change comes easily to them. They strive for it. They blossom in it. I daresay Charles would say that I blossomed too, in my own way. But it was a far more painful blossoming for me, and that is something he will never understand."

"Thank you, Mr. Hartford," Pip said quietly. "I...I may take you up on your offer some time."

"Please do," Mr. Hartford said with a small smile. He got up and picked his books off the floor.

As Mr. Hartford reached for the door again, Pip said without looking at him, "Is it so very obvious?"

He felt a tentative hand on his shoulder, but Mr. Hartford did not say anything. Pip pinched the bridge of his nose, frustrated that he could now add Mr. Hartford to the ever-growing list of people who had seen him cry.

"As I said before, Mr. Standish," was the quiet response, "I am of the opinion that you are a very brave man. I hope you recognize that too."

Pip didn't, of course, but he nodded and hunched forward.

Mr. Hartford, either out of discomfort in seeing another person's emotions or out of consideration, left the room without another word.

When Pip looked up, he noticed that the young gentleman had left a handkerchief on the desk for him.

CHAPTER 7

THE DAYS WENT by with Pip helping out in the shop more and more. He discovered accidentally that when he flashed the same smile with customers as he had with marks that the customers would sometimes buy more spells, with the hopes of another smile. Pip always accommodated. It was a strange feeling, to discover he could apply some of the same skills to his new line of work.

He was unsurprised to find that Gerry had noticed. She brought it up after a particularly busy day. She was hanging spell bags on the hooks while Pip swept the floor.

"Miss Allen bought quite a few spells today," she remarked.

Pip smiled to himself but did not reply.

"Do you realize that many people in town have started to buy spells for the sole purpose of earning one of your lovely smiles?"

He continued sweeping. He didn't think it was a question that required an answer.

"I believe there is a great deal of conjecture in whether you are of the masculine or feminine persuasion," she continued, unperturbed by his silence. "People love a man of mystery, you know. Unless I'm much mistaken, Pip dear, you are becoming quite a popular figure in town."

"Oh, I'm sure it isn't as serious as all that," he said at last.

She laughed. "I daresay it is. Do you know that the Berril siblings had a bet going as to which one of them you'd notice first?"

He looked up at that. "Who won?"

She snorted in a very unladylike manner. "You tell me."

He grinned and returned to his sweeping.

"I think tomorrow I might teach you how to run the till, if you have a mind to it."

The prospect of that much responsibility and trust startled him. But he said, "I have a mind to learn anything you care to teach me."

"Then again," she said, "we were just saying how we're teaching you too much all at once. Perhaps I should—it's just that you are learning it all so quickly, you know."

"Am I?"

She smiled. "Of course. You've picked up everything at the store remarkably fast, especially for someone with no background in trade or magic. It's very impressive. I keep forgetting how much you're learning."

"Really?" He couldn't help the pride her words gave him. He rather wished Lord Finlington had been there to hear them. He twiddled the broom in his hands. "That is nice to know."

"You don't think you're doing well?"

He shrugged. "Not particularly. I keep wishing I could learn it all faster."

She gave a thoughtful sort of hum and then returned to arranging spells, and he got back to sweeping. But he could feel her occasional glances in his direction.

The next day, she surprised him at breakfast by telling him they were taking the day off.

"It occurred to me," she said. "That most shops are not open every single day in the village. So why should we have to be? Besides, it is Sunday," she said. "I am not religious by nature, unless my parents are around, but many people are. So I think we should take advantage of the opportunity to not open the shop."

"Are you religious, Pip?" Charles asked conversationally. "The church is quite lovely. We'd be happy to take you there. The vicar is a charming man and I know he'd love to meet you. And there's a synagogue on the other side of the village, and a mosque in the next county. I'd be happy to provide you with transportation, and even company if you wish to go. Good heavens, you've been here for weeks now and none of us thought to ask you."

Pip shook his head. "No, s—Charles. I'm not religious either. I've never even been to a church, or a synagogue, or a mosque. I think I might practice a bit in the library some more."

"But you are meant to relax today," Miss Hartford said. "Not that I wish to discourage you from doing anything that pleased you, Pip. But you know you needn't practice every day."

"I still have a great deal left to learn," he said, feeling himself blush.

"Don't we all," Charles intoned.

"I have it," Miss Hartford said, clapping her hands. "Why don't we call on Bertie for tea? You haven't seen Bertie's house yet. Oh, it's ever so grand. That will be a nice way to avoid doing any work."

Pip felt a little embarrassed by Miss Hartford's solicitousness. "It is no matter," he said. "I'm accustomed to working every day. There were times in London where I even worked —" He felt his face grow hot as he caught himself from casually referring to his own shameful past. "I, er…I did not mean to—"

Charles patted his arm. "Pip, dear. I hope you know by now that you can safely tell us anything."

"Charles," Mr. Hartford said in a low voice.

Charles glanced at Mr. Hartford and then back at Pip. "Do forgive me, Pip. You are under no obligation to talk of anything you do not wish to. I did not mean to pry."

Pip murmured that it was nothing and then finished his breakfast as quickly as he could. Despite Miss Hartford's recommendations to the contrary, he retreated to the library. But he felt too restless to sit down. Instead, he paced the length of the library with his hands interlocked behind his neck. Why could he not simply be happy? He was surrounded by good, kind people who were doing every-thing they could to help him. He had delicious food, a comfortable bed, and no one treated him like a piece of prop-erty. It was, in a word, a dream. But every time he told himself to stop being ridiculous and just be happy about it, a voice in his head would remind him that he didn't deserve any of it.

His pacing quickened and it was starting to make him feel frantic when there was a soft knock on the door and Mr. Hart-ford leaned into the room.

"Ah, Mr. Standish. I was hoping I might find you here. I wondered if you might care for a stroll through the garden. It occurred to me that none of us have shown you that part of the estate."

Pip opened his mouth to tell him he appreciated the offer but was not in the mood to talk, but Mr. Hartford continued. "I should add, of course, that I am not seeking to draw you out or anything. I am not afraid of a little companionable silence. But the gardens are quite lovely and the weather is fine. If you have a mind to it, of course," he added hastily.

Pip hesitated and then nodded. "Thank you," he said.

Following Mr. Hartford's lead, he did not put on any of the usual articles of clothing requisite to a walk outside. "I'm sure it is the done thing," Mr. Hartford said when he waved off the footman. "But I never bother when I'm staying close to the house."

As promised, once they were outside, Mr. Hartford did not attempt to probe any conversation out of Pip. He shoved his hands into his pockets in a manner that Pip was fairly sure was not good for the clothes and led the way through the garden.

Pip allowed himself to be distracted by the sounds of birds, the smell of the grass, and the beauty of the garden. Born in a city, he was not used to seeing so many plants and flowers; his walks with Miss Hartford were always too purposeful for him to feel comfortable slowing down and looking about at leisure. But Mr. Hartford ambled casually down the path, pausing to look at or smell different flowers along the way, which gave Pip permission to do the same. The tightness in his chest loosened a bit as he allowed the sounds and smells of the garden to wash over him.

Pip kept expecting Mr. Hartford to spring a question on him or sit him down on a stone bench and prompt him to talk about his feelings. But, astonishingly, he never did. They walked through the garden and down to a lake and back; the gentleman never filled the silence with pointed questions or idle chatter.

It was blissfully restful.

When they circled back to the garden, they were greeted by Miss Hartford, who had donned her spencer and bonnet.

"There you are," she said when they approached. "I've been looking everywhere. Charles said you might be out here. And I thought—oh, good heavens, Gavin. Did you really walk all this time without your hat? You'll get a frightful burn. I shall have to make a tincture for you. I do wish—"

"Oh, do stop fussing, Gerry," Mr. Hartford said. "We haven't been gone all that long."

"It's been over an hour," she said.

"I wanted a bit of fresh air," he replied. "And Mr. Standish was kind enough to join me. Are you walking to Bertie's now?"

"I thought to. Unless you're too tired, Pip. In which case, we can certainly take the carriage."

"Not at all," he assured her. "I will be delighted to walk with you. Shall I get my things?"

She nodded and Mr. Hartford walked back up to the house with him. Once inside, Pip stopped the gentleman from going up the stairs with a hand on his arm.

"Thank you, Mr. Hartford," Pip said. "I needed that more than I realized."

The corner of Mr. Hartford's lip twitched but his expression remained solemn. "Don't think a thing of it, Mr. Standish," he said. And then he strode up the stairs without further comment.

Lord Finlington's house was even grander than Charles Kentworthy's. It was a full floor taller and there were two wings framing the main part of the house, making it look three times wider than Charles's house. Pip could see a manicured garden on one side of the house where it curved out of sight. They walked into the foyer over gleaming tiles. Pip glanced up to see painted frescoes across the ceiling. Everywhere there were huge, magnificent paintings or marble statues. Miss Hartford smiled at his evident awe as they were led into a library.

Pip was struck with a sudden gratitude for the library in his own new home. The viscount's library was two stories, with a staircase that curved up to the second level. He felt small and foolish standing amidst so much knowledge. He was so distracted by looking around him that he didn't see the viscount approaching.

"The most delightful of surprises, you darling things," Lord Finlington said, walking up to them. "Pip, dear. So good to see you again."

Pip bowed, feeling suddenly shy to be calling on the gentleman. Although he did notice that Lord Finlington looked remarkably well—not that he ever *didn't* look well—but Pip thought the country air agreed with the viscount. Then he began to wonder if people thought the same thing about him.

"I thought Pip might like to see your house," Miss Hartford said. "I've barely had the opportunity to see it myself."

"What a charming notion," the viscount replied. He led them out of the library and took them on a tour through the first floor. There was a huge ballroom, multiple parlors, and a dining room. Pip was completely turned around by the time they reached the other side of the house. He was already aware that the viscount was far above him in terms of rank and station, but the grandeur of his home put into stark relief the impossibility of Pip's admiration of the gentleman.

"I think you'll like the conservatory," the viscount said as he opened a pair of glass French doors.

It was the strangest room Pip had ever seen. The walls were made out of windows. Plants lined the room, stacked up against the windows, hanging from the ceiling, and arranged in large pots down the center. Miss Hartford tucked her hand around Pip's arm and led him to a small settee on one side of the room.

"This is lovely," she said as they sat.

"Mm," Lord Finlington said. "I quite like it. I'm only letting the house, of course, but I've rather fallen in love with the place. I shall be very sad when the time comes to quit it."

The gentleman's words made Pip feel a little hollow. He reached up and rubbed the tip of a large rubbery leaf between his fingers, hoping the others wouldn't notice his disappointment. Was the viscount really planning to leave? Was he only staying in Tutting-on-Cress because of Pip? He couldn't figure out why the idea bothered him so much. He hardly ever saw

Lord Finlington, but he always felt vaguely comforted by the knowledge that the gentleman was nearby.

"Perhaps we should have tea in here?" the viscount said.

"Yes, please!" Miss Hartford said.

The viscount beamed and left the room briefly. Miss Hartford gave a satisfied sort of sigh. "I hope Bertie never goes back to London. He's so lovely."

Pip nodded in agreement.

Lord Finlington returned a few minutes later. "The tea has been sent for," he said. "And this is for you, m'dear," he added, handing a piece of paper to Pip. Pip took it, confused.

"It is from Nell," the viscount explained. "I wrote to tell her that you were safely settled and her reply included a letter to you."

Pip unfolded the paper and stared at the words he couldn't yet read. He knew Nell had learned more than just magic from Lord Finlington, but to see such evidence of her knowledge was humbling.

Miss Hartford placed a hand on his arm. "Would you like me to read it to you?" she said in a soft voice.

He felt his face get hot with embarrassment, but he passed the letter over.

Dear Pip,

I was so relieved to learn that Bertie got you out of prison and that you are safe. Although I wish you weren't living quite so far away. Jack told me you'd been arrested and Bertie was the first person I could think of who might be able to help. I'm so glad he did. I haven't told Jack yet that you're out. I wasn't sure if he would be pleased knowing you were so far away. Bertie explained to me that you are not returning to London anytime soon and I'm not sure how to explain that to Jack. But I can, if you'd like me to. Do you have anything in particular you'd like for me to tell him? I'm sure he misses you as much as you miss him.

How are you getting on? Bertie said you are working for Gerry in her shop. If I didn't have a job I loved here in town, I'd almost be jealous. Imagine you working in a spell shop! I'm sure neither of us could have expected that to happen. I assume you're learning to do magic now and that you're learning to read, since that's how it was for me when I lived with Bertie. So I thought it would be nice to write to you and learn all about your new life in the country. I'm sure I would hate to live in the country. So I hope you're enjoying it more than I would.

I've made several friends here at the theater. I think you met them before when you came to visit. They're getting to be like family now, which is nice. I haven't had anyone I ever considered family, other than you and Patience. So it is nice to finally be surrounded by people who make me feel at home. I hope you're able to visit London soon and you can come see me.

Please give my regards to Gerry and Charles.

Nell

Miss Hartford folded the letter again and handed it back to him. Pip took it and slipped it into his pocket, avoiding the others' gaze.

When the tea came, he took his cup and sat quietly to himself, grateful when Miss Hartford and Lord Finlington started discussing a spell Miss Hartford was designing.

He was torn between so many feelings. He was accustomed to missing Nell; it was an ache he had long learned to live with. But he was not in the habit of resenting her, and he did resent her for that letter. He was jealous that she could write so much when he hadn't even learned to read, let alone write. He was frustrated by her surprise at him finding an honest job at last, even though he had been just as surprised as she was. He was angry with her for bringing up Jack and for suggesting that he missed him. He was filled with shame that the words had been read aloud. He felt too exposed with Miss Hartford knowing about Jack. And he didn't want to think about what Lord Finlington thought of him, with the reminder of what Jack had once been to him. It seemed that no matter how far away he was from Jack now, he would never be able to escape that part of his past.

Finally, he was hurt that she was now surrounded by friends and was where she belonged. She no longer needed him. She probably never did. Pip digested the fact that while he had considered Nell his best friend for most of his life, he had not truly felt close to her since she first left Jack's employ. She hadn't been there when Jack took him on as a lover, and he did not know how to tell her what that experience had been like. He felt sure that if he did try to explain it to her— and he didn't even know how he could since he very well couldn't ask someone to write such things for him—she wouldn't believe him. No one ever considered Jack's treatment of him strange, even Nell. Well, there had been one person: Lino Bowles, an attractive and popular harlot. He had once offered Pip help in getting out of Jack's clutches. But just as Pip had known following Nell to the viscount's house to study magic with her would make things worse, he knew Lino's help would only put them both in danger when Jack inevitably found him.

He dreaded the prospect of explaining how miserable he had been, only to have her inform him that he was terribly ungrateful. And here he was, living a comfortable and lavish lifestyle, and still terribly ungrateful. She would never understand how poorly he fit in his new life. It didn't entirely surprise him, but he had hoped she might have struggled in the same ways he had. But he could see that she hadn't struggled. She had fought for her education and fought for the opportunity to find her own place.

As Pip sat in the conservatory, dazed by the bright greenery, it occurred to him that Nell never had cause to believe she didn't deserve everything about her new life. For that reason alone, she would never understand his own sense of isolation.

"We're not the same, Nelly," he whispered to himself.

"What was that, m'dear?" Lord Finlington said.

Pip looked up in alarm; he hadn't meant for his companions to hear him. All he wanted to do in that moment was to crawl into his bed, but that was miles away now, and he didn't know his way back. He said, "I'm sorry. I didn't mean to interrupt. I was wondering if you could give me directions home? I believe I have a headache coming on."

As he might have expected, they both fussed over him after that. Miss Hartford tutted about her brother's bad influence in taking Pip on walks without appropriate headgear. A quarter of an hour later, he and Miss Hartford went home in the viscount's carriage.

At home, Jennings closed the curtains in the bedroom and helped Pip undress so he could lie down for a nap. Pip lay in bed, feeling utterly sick of being so miserable all the time. Thankfully, no one seemed to expect him to come downstairs because Jennings brought him trays for lunch and dinner. He felt wretched for causing such a fuss, but he couldn't quite bring himself to be around people either. He stayed huddled under the covers in the dark room, contemplated his many, many faults. When he finally slept, he was plagued by dreams filled with unpleasant memories.

CHAPTER 8

THE NEXT MORNING, everyone was exactly as solicitous as he feared they would be. He did not, however, expect Miss Hartford to order him to stay at home. Despite his protests, she set off for the village without him.

He felt horribly guilty, for he knew himself to not really be ill, only miserable. In an effort to assuage his own guilt, he hid away in the library and went at his letters with grim determination. Nell's letter felt like a weight in his pocket, adding to his motivation and his frustration in equal measure.

He was doing quite well for a time, and noting his own progress started to cheer him. He begged off joining the others for lunch and continued his work in the library, pausing only to rest and stretch his hand when it cramped up.

It was a very simple thing that set him off, really. He forgot to blot out the excess ink on his pen and he splotched ink all over the paper. He had done it before and moved along. But this time it was more than he could bear. He set the pen down, folded his arms on the desk, and sobbed into the crook of his elbow.

It was all too much. He couldn't do it. He had failed them. They didn't know it yet, but that made it even worse. He failed them just as he had failed Nell time and time again. She hadn't left him behind, not really. He had chosen to stay behind because of his own cowardice, and that choice had punished him for years.

He was not brave like Mr. Hartford seemed to think. He wasn't brave like Nell. Nell was off having exactly the life she was meant to have, doing grand things; no matter how hard he tried, he knew he'd never catch up to her. Now he was trapped all over again. Trapped by favors he couldn't repay, trapped by all of the things he had never learned. He didn't deserve his new friends' patience. He didn't deserve their respect or their kindness or their fine clothes. He didn't deserve *them*. Lord Finlington had been perfectly right to reject Pip all those months ago when Jack had offered him up. Perhaps he had seen Pip's myriad failings even then. He wasn't good enough for any of it.

He cried until he was gasping for breath, until his head truly began to ache, and until he had entirely forgotten what had started the tears in the first place.

He heard voices outside the door and tried to quiet himself. The last thing he wanted to do was explain everything to someone who wouldn't understand. But when Mr. Hartford slipped into the room, he found he was relieved.

Mr. Hartford did not comment on his tears or the ink splotch that Pip now realized had stained his coat sleeve. Without a word, he ushered Pip to sit on the sofa at one end of the room.

"I've asked for tea to be brought in," he said.

Pip rubbed his nose with the back of his hand. "I'm sorry."

"Don't be. The tea should help."

Pip nodded and they sat in silence until a maid brought in a tea trolley. He wondered idly if all toffs laid handkerchiefs over their teapots and, if so, why they bothered.

Mr. Hartford poured him a cup and handed it to him. "Drink first, talk after, all right?"

Pip sipped the tea, avoiding meeting the other gentleman's grave stare. When he had finished the first cup, Mr. Hartford gently took it away and set it aside. Then he passed Pip a handkerchief, folded his hands on his lap, and said, "Even if it doesn't make sense. Even if you know it to be nonsense. Even if I won't understand it. Talk it out. It may help."

And because he was so tired of keeping everything in, Pip did. It all poured out of him like an overturned teapot. He took care to leave out any mention of Jack and was circumspect in his explanation of how Nell had come in and out of his life before. But he explained his worries that he didn't fit in, that he didn't deserve their kindness, that he couldn't repay the ever-mounting debts in his life, that Nell had outpaced him, that Nell fit in where he didn't, that these realizations about Nell made him feel incredibly lonely, that he was having such difficulty in learning everything, that he disliked magical theory, and he concluded with the ink splotch and how it had devolved from a simple error into such a grand mess.

Mr. Hartford listened without interrupting, and without any pitying smiles. He just sat and took it all in with his customary solemn expression. When Pip was done, Mr. Hartford poured him another cup of tea.

When Pip finished it and set down the empty teacup, Mr. Hartford finally spoke. "I know I've already told you, but I truly do not presume that you and I have had similar experiences in life, Mr. Standish."

"I know."

"But I know how it feels to see myself as undeserving and indebted to another for kindness."

Pip looked up at him. "You do?"

Mr. Hartford nodded. "And because I know, I recognize that it will not help for me to explain to you that you are mistaken. No one can make you believe what you have already convinced yourself is true, particularly in regards to yourself. You must be the one to change that perspective. And," he said, "let me assure you, Mr. Standish, it is only that. It is a perspective. It is not the truth, but merely a part of the truth. I will not try to persuade you of your own worth. But I will tell you something my sister once told me when I was grappling with a very similar sentiment: if you trust someone, and trust their judgment, then that should extend to trusting their opinion of you. You have placed an inordinate amount of trust in us already. But if you believe us to be people of good character and sound judgment, then you might consider that we are not entirely mistaken in our assessment of you. We all believe you to be worthy."

The door opened again and Pip looked up, expecting the maid to collect the tea trolley. Instead it was Charles.

"Everything all right?" he asked as he quickly crossed the room.

Pip gave a watery laugh. "Do you always enter a room with that question?"

Charles smiled, crouching in front of Pip. "I do when I'm concerned about someone who is in it." He started to reach for Pip's arm and then stopped himself. He glanced at Mr. Hartford briefly before turning back to Pip. "My dear," he said. "I confess I've been—we've been trying to be careful about touching you too much. We all know a little of your history and, as I understand it, you may now have an unpleasant reaction to it."

Pip buried his face in his hands. "Oh, God. What did Nell say?"

"It…wasn't Nell."

Pip considered a moment and then it dawned on him. "Lord Finlington," he said, mortified.

"Had you forgotten about that conversation?"

"I will never forget it," Pip said. "I remember all of those conversations." He hesitated, peeking up at Charles, and then because he felt he had to be sure said, "I also haven't forgotten that I was in the group who was meant to rob you at Smelting's. But I think you might have."

Charles smiled. "No, I have not."

Pip groaned. "What you all must think of me. How can you be so nice to me, Charles? You know you might have died that day? It was Nell who saved you, not I. I deserve none of your kindness."

"Is it not just a little bit possible," Charles said, "that you could not save me because you were still struggling to save yourself?"

Pip did not know how he had so many tears in his body. He was grateful to already be holding a handkerchief. But he was surprised when Charles sat on the sofa between him and Mr. Hartford and gently pulled Pip against his chest. It was the first time anyone had touched him with more than their fingertips since he had arrived. And though he was grateful for their restraint, he hadn't realized how much it had added to his loneliness.

Pip gripped the lapels of Charles's coat, buried his face in the gentleman's shirt, and cried, feeling embarrassed but knowing he was too far gone to stop. Charles held him, rubbing his back. Pip was relieved that he didn't touch his hair. That would have felt too raw.

"What that man did to you, Pip," Charles said quietly, "was unforgivable. How he treated you, for I don't even know how long, was despicable. Whatever he told you, he told you only as a means to control you. You must understand that. You are worth far more than whatever that man made you believe. Do you hear me? He was wrong, Pip. He was wrong about you."

Pip sniffed, feeling overwhelmed by Charles's words. He could think of nothing adequate to say in response, so instead he said, "How can one person cry so bloody much?"

Charles chuckled and shifted so Pip's head nestled against

his shoulder. Then he took out his own handkerchief and dried one side of Pip's face. Pip noticed that Mr. Hartford was leaning against Charles's back, his head resting on the man's other shoulder.

Finally, Pip pulled away and dried the other side of his face with the handkerchief in his own hand. He said, "I rather thought you all might think less of me if you knew about...all that." He took a shaky breath. "Have you really known all this time?"

"Bertie told me that very night about the meeting with your...employer. I've never seen him so angry. He was properly horrified by the man's behavior."

"Well, I daresay he was the only one," Pip said, before blowing his nose. He felt a little buoyed to have his theories on the encounter confirmed. "I can't remember another time when someone rejected Jack's offer on principle."

"He did it often?" Charles said carefully.

Pip nodded, chewing his lip. "There was even a... customer who set up a regular weekly appointment for months." He grimaced at the memory. "Of course, Jack preferred having me for himself, but he wasn't one to pass up the chance to get some extra coin instead. He—"

He broke off at the stunned look on both men's faces. They were not, however, the expressions of disgust he had expected. Nor did he find pity, exactly. He realized that the two men looked sad, even pained, for his sake.

He leaned back against the arm of the sofa. "I've been completely terrified that you all might learn of that. I was certain you wouldn't want anything to do with me. I have so much to be ashamed of. But...is it strange I'm a little relieved that you know about it at last?"

"Not all that strange, I think," Charles said.

Pip considered this surprising shift. He continued to chew his lip thoughtfully.

Charles tapped Pip's chin with his finger. "You're abusing

that poor lip, darling." He frowned suddenly. "When was the last time you ate, Pip?"

"Breakfast."

Mr. Hartford stood abruptly. "Good God. You really will get the headache."

Charles smiled and tucked his hand under Pip's arm, pulling him up. "He's right. Let's get you some food."

After eating, Pip did not return to the library. He suspected that Mr. Hartford and Charles intentionally distracted him to keep him from doing so. They settled in one of the sitting rooms and talked for hours. To Pip's surprise, the dukex joined them, taking the other half of the sofa that Pip was sitting on. For a while, they all compared and contrasted what they each knew of London. It was strange to find some things in common with three such people. Granted, their experiences in London were vastly different from Pip's, but he had been curious all his life about the goings on of the upper classes, and his companions gladly supplied him with descriptions. Mr. Hartford's descriptions tended to be more cynical, which amused Pip greatly.

Miss Hartford arrived home early that day. Pip wasn't sure if it was because she was worried about him or because she didn't have him to escort her, but either way he felt a tinge of guilt. She didn't seem upset, however, and she seemed to notice the change in atmosphere in the house almost as soon as she had entered it. She joined them in the sitting room until dinner was ready and the conversation continued to ebb and flow more naturally than it had since Pip entered the house. He could tell the other four were being fastidiously careful about what they discussed and making sure he could take part in the conversation. Any time he was quiet for too long, they would change the subject so that he might join in.

After dinner, Mr. Hartford asked a little shyly if he knew any poetry. When Pip confessed that he didn't, Mr. Hartford brought a few volumes from the library and read to the group in the sitting room. Pip leaned back on the sofa he was sitting on, listening to Mr. Hartford's recitations. Charles read some selections as well. The dukex did not volunteer to read aloud, but they joined in the discussion of the poems and encouraged the two men to read more pieces. Pip noticed that Miss Hartford did not seem quite as enthused by poetry as the others, but he found he rather liked it. He enjoyed the rhythmic quality of the lines, and he closed his eyes and let the words float about him.

He soon fell asleep, and his mind went to the same dreadful place it often went to at night. He was awoken by someone shaking his shoulder gently. He started at the realization that he had fallen asleep, but the dukex stilled him with a hand on his chest.

"It's all right," they whispered. "It was just a dream."

The room had darkened, only dimly lit by the fire. He looked around and saw Charles crouching in front of him, looking concerned. Mr. and Miss Hartford were no longer in the room.

Pip passed a hand over his face. His heart was hammering in his chest. He wondered if the dukex could feel it.

"Do you get them often, poppet?"

Pip nodded.

"I can see about getting something to help you sleep, if you would like," Charles offered.

"Thank you," Pip said. "I think that would help." He hesitated. "Do you think it would keep me from dreaming too?"

Charles looked sad. "I'll ask."

They both helped Pip up and guided him to his room. He was very groggy, but he stayed awake long enough for Jennings to undress him and help him into bed.

CHAPTER 9

THE NEXT MORNING, Pip was acutely aware that a shift had taken place in the house. He could not be sure if it was merely a reflection of his own shifting perspective or if everyone else had experienced a change as well. When he arrived in the breakfast room, there was less shyness and awkwardness than there had been on previous mornings.

At the shop, Gerry showed him how to run the till as promised. Pip was nervous to be in charge of the money and he was greatly surprised that she would trust him with such a thing. But he felt comforted having her standing at his elbow the whole time. By the end of the day, he realized she had gradually worked her way across the store.

When she flipped the sign on the door, she congratulated him on a job well done.

"It was very...kind of you to let me work the till, Gerry," he said. "But I hope you know you do not need to. I'm frankly surprised that you trust me with such a responsibility."

She blinked at him. "Why?"

He stared. "I was a thief for all my life."

"Yes, but that was pickpocketing, wasn't it?"

He nodded.

"You never worked at shops and stole the money?"

He shook his head.

"And," she continued, walking to the back room, "as I understand it, you worked as a thief because it was the only option you had available."

He sighed and followed her. "I suppose that is true, in a way. I have a difficult time telling myself that, though. Nelly made options for herself…she even tried to persuade me to go with her. Did she tell you that?"

"She did, yes. But the first time, as I understand it, was years ago. You were both quite young."

"She was younger than I," he said.

"You were frightened, Pip. Leaving the safety of your employer was a very bold move on Nell's part. You cannot blame yourself for not taking it too."

He let out a long breath. He fetched the broom but paused at the curtain to the shop. "The fact is," he said, twiddling the broom in his hand. "I did try. I never did tell Nelly. But…"

"What happened?"

He shrugged. "I was told it wasn't an option."

"Is that what Nell was told too?"

He shook his head. "She was different." He paused. "I never told anyone. I was always ashamed, you see. I had been too cowardly to accept the opportunity the first time and then it took getting arrested to really be given another opportunity. At any rate," he said, straightening, "I thought I should tell someone about it, at last. I found myself…talking more yesterday and it helped far more than I thought possible."

Gerry gave him a bright smile. "I'm so glad you've found you can talk to me, Pip."

He turned to go to the front of the shop.

"And for what it is worth," she said, "I do not think you are a coward. Quite the opposite, actually."

When he arrived at home, Charles pulled him aside. "Bertie made this," he said, holding up a small bottle filled with light purple liquid. "Take it before you go to bed. A capful should be sufficient. Let me know when you need more."

Pip accepted the bottle. That night, he slept and didn't dream.

The next evening, he went back to practicing his letters after dinner, picking up the pen for the first time since the dreadful ink splotch. He was unsurprised when the dukex came in. He put away the pen, prepared to be told to go to bed.

But they held up their hand and said, "It's early yet, poppet. I want to see how you are doing. Do you mind?"

That did surprise him, but he shook his head and allowed himself to be led to the sofa.

"How are you getting on, child?"

"With the lessons?"

"We can start with those, if you'd like."

Pip was taken aback. "Did you mean something else, Your Grace?"

"Not necessarily," they said with a small smile. "But I suspect the lessons are not wholly separate from everything else that is troubling you. It's as good a place to start as any."

Pip shrugged. "I wish I could learn it all faster. I feel as though I am letting everyone down with my slow progress."

"There is no deadline to learning, child, no race or competition."

Pip didn't feel comfortable admitting that he did seem to be in a race, albeit a losing one, every time he compared his own progress to Nell's. So instead he said, "Miss Hartford told me it would be a great help to her if I knew how to read and write. I feel as though I am not being as helpful as I'd like to be."

"She told me that you started learning how to run the till."

He nodded.

"It does not sound to me as if you are a burden to her. You

are eager to learn and eager to help. I assure you she is not feeling impatient with you."

"I think that has more to do with her being kind, Your Grace."

"Does it matter?"

Pip was struck by the question and was silent for a long moment as he puzzled through it. Finally, he said, "I suppose I've learned to be wary of kindness, Your Grace. I prefer to earn things than be given them outright."

"An understandable sentiment, given your history."

Pip felt his face flush. "Oh. You know about that too?"

"A little. Charles warned all of us off of physical contact, for fear of distressing you."

Pip ran a hand through his hair. "It was kind of him, but I rather wish…he hadn't needed to. I mean, it is lowering that you all know everything."

"I don't know everything. Charles told us that you had been living with a person who was unkind to you and due to him, you might not like being touched. Bertram asked me separately to keep an eye on you and ensure you were given space. And I have drawn some of my own conclusions from your behavior and the way you speak of yourself."

Pip glanced up at them. "Oh." He paused. "May I ask what your conclusions were?"

The dukex smiled and leaned back on the sofa. "When I was younger, I married a person who seemed very kind. He told me he loved me, and I believed it. I was…very naive. He was cruel, really. But he was clever too, and never showed his cruelty to others. So when I confided in friends and family, they dismissed my concerns. They scolded me for speaking ill of so good a man." They shrugged. "I began to doubt myself. Before long, I no longer trusted my own judgment about anything. In the end, I was fortunate. He died five years into our marriage, when Bertram was little more than an infant. But I had spent so long not trusting myself that I could no longer trust my own grief or my own happiness. It was years before I had the courage to be happy again."

They smiled and reached up to rub their thumb lightly on Pip's cheek. "You are so young. I can only imagine how young you must have been when you met him. I am sure the man you are now would make very different decisions than the ones you made years ago. You do not need to give penance for the wrongs other people did to you. You are allowed to be happy."

Pip was not exactly surprised to be crying, but he was mildly annoyed that he could now add the dukex to the ever-growing list of people who had seen him cry.

The dukex gently pulled Pip's handkerchief out of his pocket and wiped his face. "You are allowed to cry too, you know. There is no shame in it."

"I feel as though everyone has seen me cry at this point."

"I used to hate crying in front of others. It is difficult to be vulnerable when you've spent years shielding yourself from your own unhappiness."

Fresh tears fell at this validation of his own unspoken thoughts. The dukex wiped those as well. It made Pip feel like a small child and he shivered a little at the realization; he had been thoroughly miserable when he was younger.

The dukex tucked the handkerchief back in Pip's pocket. "Answer me truthfully, child. Do you think less of me for my own mistakes?"

"Of course not," he said without hesitation.

"Even with my wealth, my property, my title, and my large family—even with all of those privileges, I still made an error in judgment that took me years to heal from. If I am permitted to make such a mistake, can you not do the same for yourself? You had far less than I did: fewer resources, fewer friends. You did what you needed to do to survive." They cupped his chin gently. "I do not think less of you for your mistakes. Forgive yourself, poppet. Give yourself permission to be happy."

Pip pulled his handkerchief back out and wiped his eyes. "I'm not even sure I know how, to be honest."

"Like most things in life, it can be learned," they said with a warm smile.

"May I ask…" Pip hesitated.

"You can ask me anything you like."

"How did you learn to be happy again?"

Their smile broadened and they considered the question. "It was a gradual process. I think what helped the most was when Bertram's mother asked me to help her manage the estate when her husband died. I moved in with them and became a part of their family. It was an extraordinary experience." They chuckled. "To put it more simply, I let people back in and trusted myself to love again."

Pip took a deep breath. "Thank you, Your Grace."

They held out their arms and said, "If it will help."

Pip folded himself forward and the dukex wrapped their arms firmly around him. They cupped the back of his head, startling him at first, but when they did not move to stroke through his hair, he relaxed. He realized as he buried his face in their shoulder, that the dukex's gentle, parental spirit had been more comforting than he expected.

Before he could talk himself out of it, he said quietly, "I never knew my parents."

The dukex rubbed his back gently. "I suspected as much. You are not lacking for friendship here, you know. I can tell you with certainty that Bertram is anxious to see you happy, as is Charles, and the Hartfords. If you were to consider us your family, poppet, I know we'd all be pleased as anything." They took a breath. "Do you know, I got to see Charles and Bertram grow up? I had a hand in raising them. I love them both like they are my own. The little Hartfords come from a decent-sized family, but I can't deny I've enjoyed taking them both under my wing. I know they don't need me, but I like to think I've helped them in my way."

Pip did not know where the dukex was going with the monologue, but he was enjoying the sensation of being held with no expectations in return, so he sat silently and listened.

"I love taking care of young people, giving them what they need to flourish. I would be delighted to bestow the same to you, if you wish it." Before Pip could respond, they continued. "And that is an offer without demands or debts, poppet. You needn't answer now, but think about it. All right?"

Pip took a shaky breath and nodded. The dukex shifted a little, and Pip felt them press a soft kiss to his head.

After a long moment, Pip pulled back. He rubbed his eyes. "I should probably go up to bed."

"Probably for the best, child. It's been a rather exhausting week for you, I think." They tucked a hand under Pip's elbow and walked him up to his room.

After he was in bed, Pip lay awake, thinking about the dukex's offer. He wanted rather desperately to accept it, and, as the dukex had advised, let them all in. He was reasonably sure none of them would hurt him as Jack had done. While he kept circling back to the argument that Jack had once seemed kind too, it seemed unlikely that all of the people he now knew were similarly duplicitous. He thought too of what the dukex had said about how young he'd been when he'd met Jack and how he would make different decisions now. Perhaps, with such experiences as he had, he had better judgment than he realized.

He took a capful of the purple liquid and lay back against the pillows, allowing himself to imagine, just briefly, what it might be like if he trusted his new friends with his heart.

~

As the weeks passed, Pip took over the till more and more regularly. Gerry started spending more time with customers, then coming back to check on him. Her trust frightened him, but he felt a determination to deserve it. So he worked diligently and the blisters on his hands turned to callouses.

After dinner, the reading lessons continued, and Pip slowly started reading the texts Miss Hartford presented him. The magic lessons did not go as smoothly. Pip felt sluggish and foolish in the face of all the names and theories and facts. When she started bringing calculations into the mix, he got so confused he wanted to cry.

Miss Hartford gave no indication that she minded his slow progress. She was patient and repeated everything as much as he asked, but he still felt like he was retaining nothing about magic. He suspected Lord Finlington had been mistaken in his assessment of Pip's talents.

One evening, the viscount himself interrupted their lessons. Miss Hartford had been showing him a diagram illustrating Pechard's Theory of Equitable Mass and explaining it for what felt like the hundredth time. Pip was staring at the diagram, leaning his head on his hands and gripping his hair tightly as if it might help his brain absorb the information better. When he heard the knock on the door, Pip didn't even look up, still puzzling over the diagram.

"Good evening, m'dears. How are the magic lessons coming along?" Lord Finlington said as he entered the library. Pip jumped at the viscount's voice. Lord Finlington strolled into the room, wearing a beautiful grey suit that seemed to Pip the same shade as the gentleman's eyes, and carrying his walking stick.

"We're muddling through, Bertie," Miss Hartford said. "I've never taught anyone else magic before. I don't know that I'm doing a good job of explaining the theories."

Pip felt himself flush at her taking all of the blame. He wanted to assure her that it was all his fault, but he was too uncomfortable to do so in front of the viscount. His cowardice made him feel even worse.

Lord Finlington did not seem to notice Pip's discomfort. He frowned slightly and came to stand next to Pip's chair, leaning over his shoulder to look at the diagram. "Hm," he said. "I've often found Pechard overblown in his own explanations of theories. He does so relish making everything complicated."

"I know," Miss Hartford said, tilting her head to look at the diagram. "But magic always comes more easily to me when I know the theory behind it first. And it's how you taught Nell, I thought."

"Yes, it is." The viscount tapped his walking stick on the carpeted floor absently. "I wonder," he said at last, "if our Pip might do better with a more practical approach."

Pip tried to ignore the warmth that burst in his chest at the gentleman's use of the word "our."

Miss Hartford frowned. "You mean I shouldn't teach him theory?"

"I mean...you might reconsider teaching him theory first." He pulled up a chair and sat down at the table with them. "If you don't mind my saying, Pip dear, I'm under the impression that you are a person who learns by doing, if you take my meaning."

Pip didn't and his confusion must have shown because the viscount continued. "Of course, darling, I don't mean to suggest you aren't terribly clever. After all, you did that travel spell with aplomb."

Miss Hartford drummed her fingers on the table. "You're right, Bertie. Do you know, I've been wondering about that. How did you teach Pip the travel spell?"

The viscount shrugged. "I performed it for him once and then showed him what to do the second time. If there had been an opportunity to perform it again, I would have given him less direction the next time."

"And that's a proper way to teach him? Pip's my first student, you know, and I'd hate to be a backwards teacher."

Lord Finlington chuckled. "Gerry, darling, positively everything about you is unconventional. Why should your teaching style be any different?"

Miss Hartford threw back her head and laughed. "What a marvelous thing to say, Bertie! How I love when you come to visit."

"I do try, my sweet. I do try."

CHAPTER 10

THE NEXT DAY, Miss Hartford informed the household that she and Pip would return home later than usual. Charles responded immediately that they would hold dinner until the two returned home. The exchange was so smooth that Pip suspected the two had discussed it in advance.

Their day at the shop was unexceptional, except that Pip noticed Gerry leaving him alone in the shop more frequently throughout the day. He realized by lunchtime that she was restocking spells as the customers were buying them, rather than doing it all after shop close. He wondered vaguely why Gerry had thought they would return home later than usual when she was saving so much time.

But it became clear when Gerry flipped the sign on the door, turned to him and said, "Let's do our magic lessons here tonight. Would you be so kind as to fetch one of the levitation spells and bring it to the work room?"

He did as she requested and she pulled all of the ingredients out onto the work bench.

"Levitation spells are fairly simple, as a rule," she began. "They do not require a great many ingredients. This one requires a feather—which you may recall from a previous lesson has the Constitutional Property to make things weightless—as well as a bit of chalk and the instructions. The chalk allows us to draw a circle to help contain the magic. That way we don't accidentally make everything float. It will also enable us to write out a sigil. The sigil will instruct the magic on how to behave. Does that make sense?"

"I believe so."

She placed the feather in the center of the workspace, along with a small book, chalked a circle around both, and then chalked some symbols into the circle. "There. This tells the magic to only levitate the book."

Pip wanted to ask why the magic didn't make the feather levitate too. But he felt sure this must have been something Gerry had explained in a prior lesson, so he didn't quite dare.

She gave him a long look. "Let's pause for a moment so you can ask me questions."

He glanced up at her. Her face held no judgment, only her usual expression of patient understanding. Seeing her across the workbench in her apron made him feel as though he were a customer buying a spell. She was, he realized, *Gerry* still and not Miss Hartford. He took a deep breath. "Is there a reason the feather does not float as well?"

She beamed. "Excellent question. And yes, there is. You might recall the lesson on how everything has the ability to be impacted by magic? Well, that is because everything has magic in it, to a degree. This feather, this book, that cut of reed, the ink well, my earrings. The sigil for this spell is essentially instructing the magic in the feather to impact the book. This little squiggle here is specifying that the Constitutional Property we are employing is the feather's lightness of weight. So this sigil is using a little of the magic from the spellcaster and taking that magic to extract the weightlessness of the feather and infuse it into the book, making the book float."

Pip considered. "Does the feather have other...erm...

Constitutional Properties that could be used in different spells?"

She looked delighted. "It has many! Did you have a spell in mind?"

He shifted his weight. "The travel spell Lord Finlington did?"

"Excellent example! It is actually being used in a similar way. In the case of a travel spell, it is making the carriage— and all its occupants—weigh less so the horses are not burdened by the weight."

Pip let out a long breath. "Oh," he said at last. "I've been wondering about that."

"Any other questions?"

He shook his head. "Not yet, I don't think."

"Let's give it a go then."

She cast the spell, explaining as she went. By the time they left the shop a little over an hour later, Pip was able to cast the spell with Gerry's guidance.

Pip found it easier to learn in the space where he spent most of his day. He liked that he learned from Gerry when they were both still in their aprons. With the additional counter space in the workroom, they managed a system for their lessons. Gerry would assemble a spell and, as Lord Finlington had done, would explain each component as she placed it, describing why it was used, detailing the orientation and placement, and explain why it all mattered. Her descriptions of the sigils were more detailed than Lord Finlington's had been, and Pip was always a trifle confused by them, but she would also show him precisely how to draw each one. He would watch her cast the spell, deactivate it, then demonstrate how to clean the workspace. Next, Pip would repeat the whole process with Gerry standing next to him and telling him what to do.

They reached a pattern for the lessons where Pip would learn a new spell on one day, and repeat the same one for several days after until he could complete the entire thing without Gerry's direction. After he had the spell down, Gerry would explain the theories behind the spell, the history, and the inventor, and sometimes even show him variations. Then, she would have him practice any other spells they had worked through. At this rate, he started to learn a new spell each week.

Gerry chose the spells from her shop to teach him and it thrilled Pip to no end to be able to use his knowledge in the shop every time he gained proficiency. There were many spells to learn and he felt he had a long way to go. But he no longer felt so overwhelmed by how much he had to learn; he began to feel excited by it.

One of the spells she taught him was one of her own design. It was an extension of a heating spell, which he had already mastered. Pip finally learned why the teapots were so often covered with handkerchiefs; the handkerchiefs had been used as the spell's focus so they might keep the tea warm. It was, Gerry explained, one of the first spells she designed by herself. Charles had been so impressed that he had all his spellcasters on staff learn the spell. Thus, throughout the house, tea could be enjoyed at leisure.

Magic lessons weren't the only thing Pip was noticing improvement in; his reading was improving as well. He was finally able to read Nell's letter by himself, although he couldn't quite bring himself to write a reply. He tried to imagine how he would describe his new life, but every description he concocted seemed insufficient. He set the letter on his dresser and contented himself with the certainty that Nell was far too busy to miss a response from him.

He was soon able to claim being too busy to reply when one night before dinner, Miss Hartford presented Pip with a surprise in the library.

"It's your very own shelf," she said. "I've put a few books

on there that I think you can handle on your own. If you have any questions, of course, don't hesitate to ask."

Pip was awed. The shelf was practically empty; only a few books had been placed there. But he liked the thought of trying to read just those few before fretting about the multitude of books in the room. He swept his fingers across the edge of the shelf.

"Thank you, Miss Hartford," he said. "It's very kind of you."

She grinned. "They're mostly children's stories. I hope that doesn't offend. It seemed like a better choice than philosophy or history or novels. No Fordyce's sermons or anything difficult like that."

"Why the blazes would he want to read Fordyce?" Mr. Hartford said, strolling into the room.

Miss Hartford huffed. "Well, some people do, Gavin. I should like to give the gentleman some breadth to his reading options, eventually."

Mr. Hartford leaned forward to look over the volumes with a critical air. "There's no poetry on here, Gerry."

"Not everyone is a fanatic for poetry," she said.

"What happened to breadth of options?"

"I said 'eventually,'" she said, exasperated. "Come along, let's go to dinner."

She took Pip's arm and walked him out of the room, leaving her brother behind. When Pip came back after dinner to grab a book, he noticed that two slim volumes of poetry had been added to his collection.

Pip loved his little shelf. He noticed that occasionally he'd find a new book on it, and he'd often wonder which one of his companions had placed it.

One evening, he strode into the library to swap out the book he had just finished for a new one and was surprised to find Mr. Hartford and Charles already in the room. They hadn't noticed his presence and they were kissing with a sweet tenderness that made him ache.

He turned to leave, but before he reached the door, he heard Charles say, "I beg your pardon, Pip. Please don't leave on our account."

When he turned back, the two gentlemen were standing a little farther apart. Charles had his hand on Mr. Hartford's back, but it was obvious that they did not plan to continue with Pip in the room. It struck him quite suddenly that he had not seen the two men show affection since Mr. Hartford had chastised Charles for kissing his wrist in front of company. He wondered if showing affection in public was something that was considered improper for people of their status or if it had to do with their knowledge of his past.

He did not wish to keep them waiting, so he quickly swapped out his book and left the room. As he walked down the hall, he passed the dukex, who was leaning against a wall. They gave him a wink. "I'll give them another fifteen minutes."

Shortly after Pip started to gain a proficiency in reading, Charles took it into his head that Pip ought to learn to ride. Apparently, the gentleman did not like to see Pip have an open schedule. When he announced this plan, Mr. Hartford had given Pip a look full of sympathy but did not otherwise involve himself.

Pip found it embarrassing at first, trying to learn to stay on the horse without falling off and trying to remember to rise in the saddle. But he found he liked having lessons that took him outdoors, for a change. Even though his muscles ached for days after the lessons, he was not as discouraged as he had been from his early progress in reading.

He liked it all the better when Charles deemed him good enough to ride around the estate. So once or twice a week, Pip and Charles would ride out together in the evening. It became one of Pip's favorite activities, seeing the early evening light and breathing in the cool, crisp air.

The change in scenery also produced a change in his friendship with Charles. Similar to being with Gerry in the shop, it felt different to be riding with Charles, far from the house and its grandness. When they were out riding, Pip found he could talk more easily to the gentleman, more like a friend and less like his superior.

"Do you know," Pip said one day. "If you had told me a year ago that I should enjoy country life so well, I would never have believed you."

Charles laughed. "We'll make a country lad out of you yet, darling."

"There's something I've been meaning to ask you," Pip said, after they had ridden in silence for a few minutes.

"Yes?"

"It might be impertinent."

"Wonderful! Do go on, dear."

Pip ducked his head, grinning. "Well, I've noticed that you and Mr. Hartford do not often…show affection to each other. Is that a matter of propriety or are you refraining for my benefit?"

Charles smiled at the question. "A bit of both. It is not considered proper to be affectionate in company. I confess I have often been one to disregard that particular rule. Having the dukex here as a chaperone means we are expected to be proper. But even if we didn't have a chaperone, we would have acted similarly as we were also unsure if it would make you uncomfortable."

"I don't think I would mind," Pip said. "I don't wish to disrupt your way of life."

Charles chuckled. "Well, in point of fact, there is another reason too. Gavin does not like public affection quite as much as I do. We are still learning each other's tastes in that regard. But I do not like to make him uncomfortable."

Pip was awed by this revelation. "That is very kind of you not to punish him."

The statement was met with a frown. "Punish him? Why on earth should I wish to do that? I am his betrothed, not his disciplinarian."

Pip felt himself flush. "Oh," he said, flustered. "I see."

"Pip," Charles said, reining in his horse. Pip hurried to do the same. Charles gave him a long, studying look. "Did he ever punish you in such a way?"

Pip swallowed. "Well, it wasn't always a punishment. That is, I don't think it was." He chewed his lip. "You see, there were times…when I couldn't think of what I might have done to…"

"He knew you didn't like it and he did it anyway?"

He nodded.

"Often?"

He shrugged. "It was just his way. Some of the time, it wasn't all bad. But—" He broke off, embarrassed by memories.

"You know that he did it as a form of punishment?"

"There were times where it was…evident."

"You can tell me, if you like."

He looked across the field. "You know that Nell asked me to leave around the time that she did, to start doing odd jobs?"

"Yes."

"Well, a while after she left, I had gotten to thinking about it. The more I thought, the more I wanted to join her after all. So, I told Jack I wanted to leave…He said it was impossible. You see, I owed him a great deal, more than Nelly did. And it would take me ever so long to pay him back, years and years." He paused, thinking about it. "I had thought that would be the end of it. But he…well, I had to be with him every night after that for simply ages. And then at the tavern he…would pick especially busy nights and—"

"Oh, Pip, I am sorry."

Pip shook himself. "I had often thought it was peculiar of me to dislike public affection so. I didn't know there were other people who didn't care for it."

"Even if it was peculiar, dear, your preferences should never be used against you in such a way. I hope you realize that?"

Pip considered this. "It was complicated. I'm not giving all of the details and I daresay I'm painting a much grimmer picture of the man than he deserves. You see, I owed him my life. He picked me up out of the gutter and trained me and fed me and housed me. He made sure I always had food and a place to sleep, even when I wasn't earning it. And..." He hesitated but soldiered on. "When Nell left, well I was so frightfully lonely. He...he saved me then, too. I knew a little of what was expected of his lovers. After all, I had known him most of my life. So, it wouldn't have been fair for me to object. It was his right, even if I didn't enjoy it."

"Is that how he explained offering you up to other people?" Charles said softly.

"Yes. I always got a cut of the pay afterward. Jack was always nothing if not fair."

Charles took a deep breath and let it out slowly. "I don't know that 'fair' is quite the word I would use to describe him, Pip."

"Oh." He felt he ought to defend Jack again, explain that he was only telling one side of the story. Instead, he sat with the idea that maybe Jack hadn't been as fair as everyone said. Maybe, similar to the dukex's husband, Jack had been cruel and unkind. Maybe Pip's misery had been warranted.

Charles was still silent beside him, allowing Pip to sort through his thoughts.

Finally, Pip said, "I still say it's a wonder I've taken to country life so well. But I wouldn't trade it for anything."

Charles gave him a beautiful, wide grin, one that made

Pip realize that Charles was an astonishingly handsome person. "I'm so glad, darling. I can't imagine our life here without you. You fit quite perfectly in our little circle."

Pip's jaw dropped at the statement. "I do?"

Charles laughed. "Decidedly so."

"I certainly haven't felt that way."

"I know you haven't," Charles said. "But it's true all the same."

"Thank you," Pip said. He felt as if he might cry and he very much didn't want to.

"Now, may I ask you something?"

He nodded.

"Are you ready for a gallop?"

"What?" Pip squawked.

Charles gave him a wicked grin and kicked his horse into movement. Pip was hard pressed to keep up. When he reached the house at last, he was breathless and flushed, and his heart felt light.

CHAPTER 11

EVERY SUNDAY, Pip and Miss Hartford would stay at home. For the first time in his life, Pip learned how to relax. It was as challenging a lesson as anything else he had received in Tutting-on-Cress. For weeks, he did not feel comfortable sitting for long periods and did not know what to do with himself when nothing was expected of him. He sensed that his new friends recognized this and felt himself being subtly trained into accepting long periods of leisure. Whether it was from Mr. Hartford inviting him on quiet walks around the estate, Charles suggesting a ride, or Miss Hartford adding a new book to his shelf, Pip slowly grew accustomed to the strangeness of Sundays.

One evening after forcing himself to take a slow and meandering walk through the garden, Pip walked into the house to hear music playing. He followed the sound and discovered Miss Hartford playing the pianoforte. She smiled at him as he approached, letting him know he was a welcome audience. Still, he walked up as quietly as he could, fearing the slightest sound would ruin the moment.

When she was done, he stood in awed silence before saying, "That was beautiful."

Her smile widened. "Thank you. I have missed playing."

"I didn't know you could."

"I haven't practiced for a little while," she admitted. "I've been so busy with the shop and everything."

"I can certainly understand that. Not to mention you've been teaching me almost every night."

"That too," she agreed. "But those are excuses, really."

"What do you mean?"

She skimmed her fingers over the keys. "Playing the pianoforte is a sort of accomplishment." She looked up at him expectantly.

He blinked, unsure of what the statement was supposed to mean.

"That is to say," she went on, "I learned it so that I might find a husband more easily."

"Playing the piano helps with that?" he said in confusion.

She laughed. "Well, as a nextborn, it is helpful to have as many attributes as possible when searching for a spouse. I have a small dowry and I come from a village even smaller than Tutting-on-Cress. My parents are not terribly well connected either. So I have to depend on my looks, my manners, my wit, and any other qualities I can think of."

"That...sounds like a lot of work."

"It is," she said feelingly. "And, as you can see...well, as my sister-in-law likes to put it: I had two Seasons in London and nothing to show for it."

He frowned. "Are you disappointed?"

She shook her head. "No, I'm much happier where I am now. But, well..." she sighed. "Most of my friends in London have stopped talking to me. Working in trade was a decided step down, socially. The dukex did warn me that the move would be permanent, so I was somewhat prepared for a loss in marriage prospects. But I was not entirely prepared to be a social pariah."

"I'm sorry," he said quietly.

She gave him a small smile. "I didn't think being a spellmaster was possible for me, so I barely allowed myself to dream about it. So this is decidedly a better situation for me than being married. Still, I do like the idea of romance and marriage. Now that I have a career, I have more time to find a husband, but only if I want to. So it is nice to have that security."

Pip nodded distractedly. He wondered if he was expected to marry now that he was living with a higher class of people. He found himself balking at the very notion. Then again, he wasn't sure he wanted to depend on Charles's generosity forever.

Miss Hartford began to play another song and Pip sat down to listen, letting the music sweep away his worried thoughts about being a burden.

∾

PIP SOON LEARNED THAT SUNDAYS WERE ALSO THE DAY VISITORS would come by the house. He actively avoided these for two months, as he knew practically no one in the village. But in early November, Miss Hartford invited him to join her in the sitting room.

"I am having a couple of friends over for tea," she said as he sat down.

He looked at her in surprise. "Are you sure you want me to be here?"

She smiled. "Of course, silly. I thought it might be nice for you to meet more people now that you're settled."

"Oh."

"Today, it's my cousin Rose and her wife, Julia. They'll both adore you and they're very sweet, so I'm sure you will like them too." She poured him a cup of tea. "Teatime visits are a little less formal than other social calls. They do not last as long as a mealtime. Some visits only last a half hour."

He noticed she was speaking in the same tone of voice she

used when she was teaching him magic. Realizing this was a new sort of lesson, he straightened in his seat.

When Miss Hartford's guests came he was terrified at first, for they seemed very fine. Miss Hartford introduced him by saying, "This is Mr. Standish, a friend of Lord Finlington's from London. He has graciously agreed to live in Tutting-on-Cress and work as my shop assistant. He has been invaluable." He relaxed, realizing that she had no intention of conveying his past to anyone outside their tight little circle.

Her description of him was *a* truth. Pip was not entirely comfortable with how much was omitted in that truth, but he decided to trust Miss Hartford's handling of the matter. She explained to her guests that Mr. Standish's parents had died when he was quite young and he did not know his own family; her friends were too sympathetic to this plight to inquire further, so Pip adjusted to this version of his history. It was a cleaner version of the truth, and much more palatable.

"We've wanted to meet you for months," Mrs. Julia Hearst said with a warm smile. "Gerry speaks very highly of you."

"Yes," Mrs. Rose Hearst agreed. "And it is nice to have more young people move into the neighborhood. Particularly unmarried young people."

Pip looked at her in alarm.

Miss Hartford chuckled. "Don't mind her, Pip. Rose is always up to some scheme or other. Rather like Charles," she added.

Mrs. Rose Hearst huffed in mock annoyance. "Well, I like that! But you needn't worry, Mr. Standish. I promise not to scheme on your behalf until I know you better."

Pip gave a small laugh as he accepted a slice of cake from Miss Hartford. He noticed how she turned the conversation to ask her guests about their lives, inquiring after the health of their cook, the development of some improvements on their cottage, and her cousin's siblings. After nearly an hour of conversation, he realized she changed the topic any time her guests inquired too closely into Pip's history or made a comment about her marriage prospects. It reminded him a little of Lord Finlington and how little he spoke of himself.

It occurred to him that Miss Hartford was subtly showing him how to converse with others in a way that allowed him to comfortably keep his history secret. He knew her well enough to know when she was showing him something she wished him to take note of. Duly, he took note. He also learned how to sit properly, how to accept and drink tea before company, and how conversation flowed in polite society. He learned this by example rather than by tutelage.

When the focus of conversation was not on him, he took the opportunity to observe the guests. Mrs. Rose Hearst had a strong family resemblance to her Hartford cousins: pronounced cheekbones, a narrow chin, pale skin, and small mouth. Her hair was a dark brown and her eyes were hazel. She was a striking-looking woman who talked a great deal and often with a mind to gossip or complain. But her wife and cousin took this in such good humor that Pip discerned there was little actual meanness to the woman's temperament. She also seemed to have a propensity to get into a great many mishaps and misunderstandings; Miss Hartford seemed particularly keen to draw these stories out.

Pip liked Mrs. Julia Hearst a great deal. She was a calm and quiet sort of woman who struck Pip as someone who learned more about people by observing rather than probing information out of them. She was short, curvy, and very lovely.

After their first visit, the Hearsts came almost weekly. Pip looked forward to their visits, for Rose Hearst and Miss Hartford would often sit together and gossip while Julia Hearst would talk in her calm and quiet way to Pip. He was relieved to discover that Miss Hartford tended to invite the same small group of acquaintances. He suspected she was intentionally keeping the circle small for his comfort, considering how friendly she was and how most of the village customers talked to her as if she was already a close friend.

He met Mrs. Lizzy Canterbury, Miss Kitty Corley, and the Ladies Windham. He liked Mrs. Canterbury. She was friendly, good-natured, and chatty. Pip discovered that when Mrs. Canterbury came to visit, he barely had to speak at all; she kept up a stream of conversation for nearly her entire visit, punctuated by Miss Hartford's commentary. Mrs. Canterbury had an open and frank nature that reminded him of some of the people he knew in London, which made him feel less strange in her company.

Miss Kitty Corley was exactly what he might have expected from a Nextborn of Quality. She looked like a china doll, all fragile and sweet. Jack would have found the lady very attractive, which Pip worried was part of the reason he did not care for her as much. She was also very shy, which made Pip uncomfortable, as her visits were often quiet experiences of everyone trying to find ways to fill the silence.

As for the Ladies Windham, while he thought Lady Maria Windham to be a pleasant and easygoing sort of woman, he didn't care for her wife, who was very forward and flirtatious. She would always try to sit very close to Miss Hartford and lay her hand on the other lady's knee while she talked. Miss Hartford took the flirtations with more amusement than offense, but it reminded Pip too strongly of Jack's constant desire to touch.

After the Hearsts' initial visit, the dukex often joined them. This was usually a relief, for they would deftly take control over the conversation, particularly if Pip was the focus for a long time. Sometimes Mr. Hartford or Charles would join for tea as well, and the focus would pull toward one or both of those gentlemen instead. It was common knowledge among the village that the two men were betrothed and people often wished to know if they had yet set a date. They had not, so the conversation inevitably moved on to suggestions for which date they really ought to choose, as if the reason a date had not been set was because the two gentlemen did not have a good notion of the calendar.

Gradually, the Sunday teatime visits became almost routine and he grew more comfortable with small talk and listening to idle village gossip. As Miss Hartford had first explained to him, teatime was a very specific period in the day—a few hours after lunch—so his Sundays were still mostly empty for him to fill as he saw fit. After nearly a life-time of having his time controlled by Jack, it took Pip some time to properly learn what he enjoyed doing. He found he liked spending time with Miss Hartford's friends, particularly when he was not the focus of conversation, and he enjoyed simply *being*, without worrying about what the next day would hold, or fretting about what was expected of him. This strange new freedom made him feel as if he was under-standing himself from scratch.

CHAPTER 12

ONE DAY when Pip joined Miss Hartford for tea, he was surprised to find Lord Finlington in the sitting room. He was further surprised when Miss Hartford asked the dukex for a walk in the garden, leaving Pip alone to entertain the viscount.

The dukex agreed but said, "We shall return in a half hour."

Pip couldn't tell who the statement had been intended for, but he nodded as if it were meant for him.

After they left, Pip felt the usual shyness that came upon him when he was alone with Lord Finlington. He was distracted, as ever, by noticing the way the viscount's coat brought out the grey in his eyes and how gracefully his fingers moved when he stirred his tea. Flustered by these observations, Pip cast about desperately for a conversation topic. Fortunately, the viscount, as usual, had the matter well in hand.

"How are you getting along, m'dear?" he asked.

"Very well, sir," Pip replied.

"I'm so glad to hear it. I admit, darling, I have been worried about you being unable to settle here. You will tell me, I hope, if you are ever unhappy. I assure you, I will do everything in my power to make sure you are well situated."

Pip swallowed. "That is very kind of you, my lord. I confess I do not know what I have possibly done to deserve your kindness. I think you should know that you rescued me from more than just prison in bringing me here. I don't know how I shall ever repay you."

Lord Finlington gave a small smile. "Extracting you from your previous situation was a personal goal of mine ever since our evening at the Fox & Thistle."

It was the first time the viscount had ever referenced that conversation and Pip was horribly embarrassed by it. He ducked his head and clasped his hands together. "I cannot imagine what you must have thought of me, sir."

"Oh, I don't know the best way to describe it, darling," Lord Finlington replied. "But I think I can liken it to seeing a flame being covered with a dark lampshade. Your light was so diminished when you were in that man's presence. Now, I do not wish you to mistake my concern for pity. There are a great many people in London for whom I might feel pity. But in you I saw a man who had a great strength of spirit, not to mention an absurd amount of untapped magical talent. I wished to free you from that darkness and show you how brightly you might shine."

Pip chewed his lip, feeling undeserving of such a grand comparison.

"I regret to say it took me several months, far longer than I would have liked, to think of a good strategy. I was a trifle worried you might be of the same opinion of your situation as dear Nell and that you would refuse my help. Especially when you turned down Nell's invitation to accompany her. I didn't want to press the matter for fear I might lose the opportunity to help you. So I thought it out carefully for months. It was not until I recalled something Nell told me about paying off her debt that I had a notion of what to do. I thought perhaps the reason you had turned Nell down was out of a sense of indebtedness, rather than love. In any case, I thought it best to be sure. I decided if you really did love the wretched man that at least you would have the proper choice. We only learned of your arrest because I sent Nell to pay the rascal off."

Pip was dumbfounded. "You would have paid off what I owed him? You intended to do that…for me?"

"Of course, darling. And gladly."

"I already owe you so much. I hate to imagine having that debt added to it."

The viscount gave a small sigh. "I wish I could impress upon you, m'dear, that not everyone is cut of that cloth. I have no expectation or desire for any repayment. I consider you my friend, but even that is something separate, for I would hate for you to accept my friendship out of obligation."

"I do consider you a friend, sir. I'm afraid I'm still getting accustomed to the rest. It is…quite the opposite of what I have learned throughout my life."

"I understand. Not to worry. But you did not answer my question, dear man," the viscount said. "Are you happy?"

Pip looked at him, startled. "Of course, sir."

Lord Finlington waited.

Pip considered a moment longer. "Or rather, let's say, I am learning to be happy, sir."

The viscount smiled in evident relief. "I am so very glad to hear it, darling."

Pip frowned a moment, thinking back to something the viscount had just said. "I hope you will forgive the question, sir, but what did you mean by 'an absurd amount of magical talent?' I know I have a moderate amount of magical ability, but nothing I have seen in my magic lessons has shown anything more. Miss Hartford has never said anything about it."

The viscount's smile widened. "Ah, I'm so glad you brought that up, m'dear. It is the second reason I asked Gerry if I might visit with you today."

Pip's eyes widened. "You asked to speak to me today?"

"Yes, I hope you don't mind. I wished to see how you are getting on and also discuss your magic lessons. Gerry and I have been discussing them for quite some time."

"You have?"

"Yes, darling, ever since she adapted her lessons to a more practical style. You see, Gerry is, frankly, a magical genius. She understands the theories and science of magic better than most spellcasters in the country. She has instinct for what a spell needs to be more potent. However, her experience with magic is more cerebral—that is to say, she goes at it from what she knows of it. As she knows a great deal, this is not a detriment to her. Most spellcasters are similar—they see magic as a science. They learn the theories and the diagrams and the placements and the movements until they gain proficiency. Nell taught herself because she was good at observing what people did. She discovered her little look-away spell in a manner that was, I think, part accident and part cleverness. She learned it worked by trial and error, determining when people noticed her or didn't notice her.

"You, however," he went on, "are different. You *feel* magic, which is very rare indeed. You felt the spell in the lock when you broke into the study, even though you didn't know that at the time, and you were able to maneuver the lock pick around the spell quite unconsciously. Then you not only sensed the trap I had laid, but you resisted it." The viscount shook his head. "That is, dear man, not common. For it means you can not only sense magic, but you can examine that sense too. Only a few spellcasters have that and most of them have to be trained to learn it. I have learned to sense magic, but it took years of practice and study. And even then it is still a challenge for me to not be swept up in the feeling."

Pip gaped. The viscount chuckled. "Think about the time we did those travel spells, hm? And every time you've practiced a spell since. Can you feel when the spell is active?"

Pip nodded slowly.

"And you can feel when it has been taken down?"

Another nod.

"Well, there it is," he said, as if that settled the matter.

"You mean, Miss Hartford and Nell don't feel that?"

"Well, they could, I'm sure, if they put their minds to it. As a matter of fact, Gerry and I have discussed it and she wishes to learn. I intend to teach her, but first, I intend to teach you."

Pip did not know what to say.

"It will be a learning experience for both of us. For I have never taught anyone that particular skill, besides myself. You already have the innate ability, so it will be less about learning how to do it and more about how to control and apply it."

"You're sure you don't mind, sir? I know you're very busy."

"Mind? You sweet thing, I am impatient to begin! Gerry and I have settled on a schedule. She shall continue to teach you three evenings a week, every other day. I shall take the in-between days for the more advanced lessons."

"Oh, sir," Pip said, feeling a little panicky. "I'm sure I'm not at all ready for advanced lessons."

"I think you may surprise yourself," the viscount said.

It occurred to Pip when he went to work the next day that every time he got accustomed to his routine in his new life, something happened to shake it up. He sat with that realization all day and finally came to the conclusion that he did not entirely mind it.

And so, he began the new phase of his magical education. On Mondays, Wednesdays, and Fridays, he would learn spells with Gerry and practice those he already knew. On Tuesdays, Thursdays, and Saturdays, Lord Finlington would come by the shop to teach Pip a very different form of magic.

Gerry was always present for these lessons. She assured him that she liked having time carved out for her own magical experiments. But Pip suspected her presence had been arranged in advance for his comfort. Considering how shy he felt when he was alone with the gentleman, he had to admit that her presence did make him a little less flustered. Having the whole of Lord Finlington's attention was both exhilarating and nerve-racking.

Lessons with the viscount were very strange, but Pip rather loved them. For the first two weeks in November, they ran through spells Pip had mastered. First, the viscount would perform the spell and have Pip try to describe how the magic felt. Pip would then perform the spell, trying to cast and feel the magic at the same time. It took a while to get accustomed to it, for it was a bit like doing two completely different things at once.

The more they practiced, the more it became instinctual, and Pip found that he didn't have to concentrate so much on feeling the spell. Oddly, it also made casting the spells themselves easier. Because instead of going off his eyes alone to straighten an item, he could sense when the spell was balanced as he placed the items.

After the second week, the viscount pronounced himself satisfied with Pip's progress and said, much to Pip's alarm, that they would be moving on to a certain kind of advanced spellwork. Since taking up magic lessons, Pip had learned mostly basic spells and only ones that required a set up. These were the more traditional form of spellcasting and often required sigils and incantations and exact placement, not to mention thorough clean up.

Gerry had explained to Pip that there were three kinds of spellwork: the basic ones; more complicated and fiddly spells that were cast the same way as the basic ones; and the more modern so-called Motion spells. These spells had emerged in recent years and required fewer ingredients and no set up or clean up at all. However, they were often very difficult to get right: the hand motions had to be exact, any incantations that were used had to be said perfectly, and the ingredients themselves had to be in tip-top shape. Pip learned that this form of spell casting was what Nell had taught herself back in London. It was why her castings had not been consistently successful, and as her ingredients were often not in prime condition, the magic was not as potent.

Lord Finlington started Pip on a levitation spell. It was the same spell he had witnessed Nell performing in their room, what felt like a lifetime ago. After practicing the feel of magic as he performed it, Pip was surprised how easily Motion magic came to him. He could feel when he did the hand motion correctly and he could sense the spell take hold in his hand. He progressed through these lessons with far more speed than anything he had learned since leaving London. The viscount was thrilled and began giving Pip increasingly difficult spells to perform.

The one that gave him the most stick was a wind spell.

"It is a combination of two spells you have already learned," Lord Finlington explained. "It combines levitation and lateral movement."

Both of these spells had proven to be very helpful for Pip's work in the shop, as he was able to shift boxes up and around the back room. It must be confessed that he performed the spells even when he didn't strictly need to, but Gerry always laughed indulgently and encouraged what was, to Pip's mind, excessive laziness.

"Now, we do not use a feather as with the levitation spell, nor a wood rod as with the lateral movement spell. We will be using a willow branch. The reason for the willow branch is that it contains Constitutional Properties that are used for both spells."

The viscount passed a willow branch to Pip. He had learned over the course of their lessons that Lord Finlington liked to see him take a hands-on approach to his learning. That is, he encouraged Pip to pick up the ingredients, move them around, or feel the weight of them in his hand. So Pip swished the willow branch a bit, noting the sound it made as it cut through the air and the feel of it against his palm.

"Very good, darling," Lord Finlington said.

Pip resisted the urge to beam. No matter how many times Lord Finlington complimented him or praised his work, it never failed to thrill Pip.

The viscount held out his hand to take the branch back and said, "The movement is a bit complicated for this one. You will essentially be combining the gestures of the other two spells. Doing the upward maneuver for lateral movement and twisting your wrist to indicate the direction. Like so." He demonstrated, sending a handkerchief to billow around the room.

"As with all spells, you can control the power behind it. But because this spell makes use of two separate movements, there is automatically more power in it. It is very easy to overshoot, so we will be using lighter and less breakable objects for our practice. And you will have to temper that power as we've discussed." He looked at Pip expectantly.

"With tighter wrist movement, more focus, and...er... calm?" Pip recited.

"Exactly, m'dear. Excellent memory. And, of course, control will come in time. So don't fret if it doesn't come easily now. Let us begin, shall we?"

As much as he had learned to master the two original spells, combining them proved very tricky. He could feel the spell activate and he could sense that the magic in it was strong, but he struggled to adjust the power behind the spell. After a week, Lord Finlington pronounced himself satisfied and moved them on to a new spell, but Pip was frustrated by his own lack of control and continued to practice when he was alone in the garden. He wanted to do better than simply meet the viscount's expectations; he wanted to surpass them.

Although once when he was practicing, Mr. Hartford strolled by and commented, "You know I've always felt as though Motion spells are beyond me."

Pip stared at him in surprise. "Really?"

"I don't quite like the idea of doing magic so *openly*."

Pip picked up the pillow he had been practicing with. "I suppose after working in the shop, magic feels like the sort of business one does openly. I only do it alone when I'm practicing."

"Are you enjoying it?"

"Yes, much more than when I first started. And actually I think I like Motion spells better than Traditional ones."

Mr. Hartford's mouth twitched. "I'm glad you're enjoying it. Perhaps I ought to give it a try after all."

"Both your sister and Lord Finlington have said you're very talented with magic. It would probably help you when you're trying to get a book off a particularly high shelf."

Mr. Hartford gave a surprised sort of laugh. "That's as good an inducement as any. Thank you. I shall consider it."

He walked away and Pip felt a strange sort of accomplishment from the conversation.

CHAPTER 13

Pip was surprised by how comfortably he was now settling into his new life. Most days were filled with working at the shop and various magic lessons, and most evenings involved a short ride around the estate or the household settling into the sitting room to read or talk. Occasionally Lord Finlington would join them for dinner in the evenings after the lessons were over.

One evening, Pip was taking a stroll through the garden before dinner and found Charles and Lord Finlington sitting together on a bench, talking animatedly.

"It's too soon, Charlie," the viscount was saying.

"Yes, I know. Too soon for anything serious. But it wouldn't hurt for you to visit more often."

"I *am* visiting."

"You know what I mean, Bertie. You ought to visit with more purpose. Become better acquainted with him. If I didn't know better, I'd say you were dithering."

Lord Finlington huffed. "I'm not dithering. I'm being respectful. Besides, I've already told you that I have no expectation of—"

"Oh, good evening, Pip," Charles said in a loud voice.

The viscount turned and, seeing Pip, stood and bowed. "Good evening, m'dear. Did you have a good day?"

"Yes, my lord," Pip said. "I'm very sorry for interrupting. I can—"

"Not at all," Charles said. "In fact, I really ought to go inside and take care of a few things before dinner. Why don't you keep Bertie here company until dinner is ready?" He gave Lord Finlington a pointed look, flashed Pip a broad smile and then quickly walked inside.

"Were you about to take a stroll through the garden, m'dear?"

Pip nodded.

"Well, perhaps I can accompany you?" Lord Finlington offered his arm.

Pip felt shy about the gentleman's gallantry, but his lessons with Lord Finlington had helped ease some of his bashfulness around the gentleman in general. He took the offered arm, grateful that the viscount was giving him the choice to take it. Then again, Lord Finlington had always been nothing if not scrupulously kind ever since they'd met in London. He was reminded of how Lord Finlington had been the one to tell his companions to avoid touching Pip overmuch.

Taking a deep breath, he said, "I haven't yet thanked you, my lord."

"For what, my sweet?"

Pip laughed a little. "Well, the list is so long, I'd hardly know where to begin. But I specifically meant how you…saw to it that everyone here was…respectful of my person."

Lord Finlington seemed to hesitate. "I was glad to do it, darling. But you do not need to thank me. Respecting your person is the very least any of us could offer you. It barely warrants as a kindness, to my mind. But rather basic courtesy."

Pip shook his head. "In my experience, it's a little too

much to expect. I'm accustomed to people feeling entitled, merely because they find me…attractive."

He glanced up at his companion. Lord Finlington looked almost embarrassed. "I fear you've experienced the worst humanity has to offer, m'dear. Your beauty, as notable as it is, does not make you less worthy of respect or dignity."

Pip gave a small smile. "I think if I were to use you as a standard to judge humanity, my lord, I would certainly find most people lacking."

The viscount reached a hand up, as if he were going to place it over Pip's own, but then dropped it abruptly. "You sweet thing," he murmured.

Pip rather wished Lord Finlington had touched his hand, but considering their topic of conversation, he was not entirely surprised by the aborted movement. There was a small lapse in conversation, then Pip said, "Are you joining us for dinner, my lord?"

"Yes. Charlie has insisted that I've become far too reclusive since coming to the country."

"Do you…prefer to be reclusive?"

Lord Finlington seemed to consider the question. "I am a social person by nature, so I don't intentionally avoid the company of others. But I do tend to get distracted by my various magical projects. I lose all sense of time, really. It has long been a habit but I'm afraid country life has exacerbated it somewhat. You see, in London, I was always busy with different dinners and parties. I had to plan my projects around my social calendar. Now it is rather the other way around."

"It sounds as if you have more time to work on your projects."

"Yes," he said with a chuckle. "But both Charlie and my cousin have been lecturing me a bit on getting a little too deeply involved in projects and neglecting…well, getting too reclusive, as I said. Of course, our lessons at the shop have given me a good opportunity to leave the house, and then I get to see you and dear Gerry. But my cousin keeps telling me that I need more company."

"Does that mean you will be dining with us more often?" Pip said, feeling a little hopeful.

"I suppose it does."

Pip drew up some courage and said, "I'm glad to hear it."

Lord Finlington's smile in response was a beautiful thing. "Thank you, m'dear. I shall be glad to see more of you as well."

Pip tried to think of something to say that would allow him to keep seeing that smile. "What are your magical projects, my lord?"

To his disappointment, the smile faded, replaced by a pensive look.

"If you don't mind my asking," Pip added hastily. "I didn't mean to pry."

Lord Finlington placed his hand over Pip's reassuringly, and Pip tried to hide how pleased he was. "Not at all, darling. I...I will gladly tell you anything you wish to know." He looked a little flustered, although Pip didn't know why. Dropping his hand away, he said, "It's a bit of a challenging project, not because of the magic involved—although that has been a delightful puzzle—but because of the...ethical aspect."

Pip frowned in confusion.

"I apologize, m'dear. I'm explaining this all backwards. I'm designing a scrying spell, which essentially allows a spell-caster to view another person or place from a distance."

Pip felt his eyes widen.

"It is something that spellmasters have been working to do for ages, so it is not an original concept of mine. And it has some definite drawbacks. For instance, the spellcaster cannot hear what is being said; they can only see. My primary concern is one of...well...consent. While the concept of being able to make sure loved ones are safe is an appealing one, many people would not want to be scried on without their knowledge or their permission. A child away at school may not want their parents to see their every move, a jealous lover could use it maliciously, and so forth."

Pip imagined what Jack might have done with such a tool and shuddered.

"Precisely," Lord Finlington said. "Then, of course, there's the matter of what would happen if the spell got into the wrong hands—an enemy force, for example. We might not want foreign governments looking at our map rooms or council chambers. So my dilemma is less about whether or not I can accomplish the task but more of whether or not I want such a spell to exist in the first place."

"Perhaps—" Pip began before he could stop himself. He felt his face get hot at his own audacity and immediately cut himself off.

But Lord Finlington turned to him inquiringly. "Yes?"

"Forgive me," Pip said. "I did not mean to be presumptuous."

"Not presumptuous at all, darling. I would love to hear your thoughts on the matter."

Pip took a deep breath. "Well, I don't know much about magic, of course. But would there be a way to make the spell only work if the person being viewed had agreed to it?"

Lord Finlington looked thoughtful and walked for a few minutes in silence. Finally, he said, "I think that could work. Perhaps if I tied the scrying spell to another one—I could use the—hm…and then, of course, it would solve…" He glanced at Pip and gave an apologetic chuckle. "I'm afraid I get into my own head with these things."

Pip tried to smile reassuringly. "I don't mind."

Lord Finlington stared at him briefly and then seemed to shake himself mentally. "At any rate, it is an ingenious suggestion, m'dear. I am grateful to you."

Pip would hardly have called the comment ingenious, but

he basked in the compliment. "I'm glad I could help. I hope it won't mean you have to start over or anything."

The viscount shook his head. "I imagine I will have to go back a few steps, but I have an idea of where to start. I think the primary challenge now will be in finding a partner for the experiment. I've been practicing on my empty study in London, you see."

Pip hesitated, then said, "Could I help?"

Lord Finlington seemed taken aback. "It is good of you to offer. But I have no desire to infringe upon your privacy."

"You wouldn't. I'm...I'm offering. That is, unless you would need me to do a spell. I'm not sure I'd be much help in that case. I'm not very good."

Lord Finlington waved his hand in a vaguely dismissive gesture. "Nonsense, darling, you have exceptional talent. It wouldn't require any spellcasting on your part. But I do hesitate to…"

Pip considered retracting the offer; Lord Finlington looked surprisingly uncomfortable with the idea. But he so liked the prospect of being of real help to the gentleman. He placed his other hand on Lord Finlington's arm. "As your friend, my lord, I would be honored to be of assistance. I trust you. Besides," he added with a self-deprecating smile, "I am not doing anything particularly interesting, so there is more danger of you being bored with me as a subject than anything else."

Lord Finlington swallowed and was silent for a long moment before saying, "Thank you, darling. I'm honored by your trust. I would...I would be grateful for your assistance."

Pip breathed out in relief.

Lord Finlington cleared his throat and resumed walking. Pip hadn't realized they'd stopped. "I shall let you know when I have an idea of how to proceed."

The dukex walked into the garden at that juncture. "There

you are, Bertram," they said. "I thought you had forgotten to join us."

"Forgive me, Your Grace. Pip was kind enough to invite me in his turn about the garden."

"So I see. Well, much as I hate to interrupt what is surely a charming conversation, dinner is nearly ready. Come along." They turned and led the way back into the house.

As they sat down to dinner, Charles said he hoped they'd had a pleasant time in the garden, to which Lord Finlington had raised an eyebrow and said, "Absurd of you to suggest that any conversation with Pip would be anything but pleasant, Charlie."

Pip couldn't resist the grin that overtook him at the compliment. When Lord Finlington changed the topic, Pip wondered if the gentleman intended to keep their conversation private, which gave him a strange sort of thrill. He liked the idea of having something private to share with the viscount. His pleasure was increased a few days later when he received a letter from Lord Finlington:

Dear Pip,

Ever since our conversation, my experiments have significantly improved. I have determined how best to proceed with your most excellent suggestion. If you have changed your mind, I will completely understand. I have no desire to pressure you in this matter. However, if you are still amenable, I will need a small token from you—a handkerchief, perhaps, or a button, or even a small note with your signature will suffice. As I understand it, giving with the intentions we discussed will be key.

Affectionately,

Bertie Finlington

He was surprised Lord Finlington had sent a note instead of asking him in person during one of their lessons, but he couldn't deny it pleased him to receive it. He read the small note several times over. He brushed his thumb over the words *"Dear Pip"* and *"Affectionately."* He was delighted that the viscount signed the letter with his first name, as if he wanted Pip to address him as such, although Pip was quite sure he didn't yet dare such a thing.

He wandered his room for nearly an hour, trying to determine what token to send. He was shy at the idea of sending a note in response, considering how poor his own handwriting was. After his seventh reread of the letter, he decided a note was necessary in order to convince Lord Finlington that he was offering the token willingly.

As carefully as he could, he wrote:

My lord,

I am happy to offer my help. As I said before, I trust you. Please tell me if you need anything else.

He stared at the small missive for a long moment before finally adding:

Your friend,

Pip Standish

When Jennings came in to help him dress for dinner, Pip asked the valet to show him how to fold the letter. Before it was sealed, Pip tucked a fresh handkerchief into the paper. Then he handed it to Jennings to be sent out.

CHAPTER 14

DECEMBER CREPT in and Pip got to experience the first comfortable winter of his life. He had never had enough layers to get properly warm when he lived in London. Now he was encouraged to indulge in soothing baths, cozy blankets were piled onto his bed, hot tea and mulled wine were readily available, warming spells were set up all over the house, cheery fires blazed in the hearths, and Charles outfitted him with clothes designed for winter. Pip felt he was truly in the lap of luxury.

On a chilly evening, Lord Finlington came by for dinner, and Charles stood at the start of dinner to make an announcement. He held up his glass and said, "My dearest friends, I would like you to be the first to know that Gavin and I have settled upon a date for our wedding."

Miss Hartford clapped her hands. "How capital!"

"Thank heavens," the dukex murmured.

"Oh, don't keep us in suspense, darling!" Lord Finlington said.

Charles grinned, paused (contrary to the viscount's request), and finally said, "We shall be married at the end of January."

Miss Hartford gasped. "A year from when you proposed? Oh, Charles, how unbelievably romantic of you!"

Charles laughed and everyone offered their congratulations. They talked of nothing else throughout the course of the dinner. Miss Hartford, the dukex, and the viscount had a wealth of suggestions for the wedding. Mr. Hartford warned everyone that it would mean his family would be visiting for the occasion.

"Oh, goodness," Miss Hartford said. "Even John?"

"He shall have to be invited," Mr. Hartford agreed. "Although God knows whether he will actually attend."

A few days later, Pip ran into Mr. Hartford as he was strolling through the garden.

"Ah, Mr. Standish," the young man said in greeting. "Don't mind me. I'm just working out some nervous energy."

Pip was surprised by the confession. "Would you like company?"

"Your company is always welcome."

They walked in silence for a few minutes.

"You said you had nervous energy?" Pip eventually asked. "Does that mean you are nervous about something or is that simply an expression?"

Mr. Hartford shrugged. "A little nervous, I suppose."

"Would you like to talk about it?"

"I'm sure you have enough troubles of your own without..." he tapered off and glanced at Pip. "Although I daresay you wouldn't have offered if you didn't mean it."

"No, I wouldn't. Are you nervous about your family coming to visit? Or the wedding, perhaps?" Pip asked.

Mr. Hartford stuffed his hands in his pockets. "I like my parents very well and my younger brother Seb is good company, although he can be a bit of an idiot sometimes. But my older brother John has a tendency to scold everyone. He always thinks he is the cleverest person in the room, you see. But you needn't worry, Mr. Standish," he went on. "I'm sure my parents will like you. Seb may try to flirt with you, I'm afraid. I'll do my best to quash that, of course. John and Veronica will likely be too focused on scolding Gerry and me that they will probably leave you alone."

"Thank you, Mr. Hartford. But I'd hate for you take the brunt of—"

Mr. Hartford waved a hand dismissively. "They're my family, Standish. I rather think it's my duty to take the brunt of their nonsense."

Pip considered the young man, realizing that for all of Mr. Hartford's kindness and patience with him, he still spoke to Pip with formality. "You can call me Pip if you'd like, sir," he said.

Mr. Hartford's mouth twitched slightly. "Thank you, Pip," he said. "Gerry's right, you know. You are practically family. I'd be pleased if you called me Gavin. Though not Gav," he added, "John calls me Gav. I've always hated it."

Pip was nervous about the prospect of meeting the rest of the Hartford family, but comforted by the certainty that he would likely be too busy in the shop to socialize much. And he was sure his friends would keep him from any unpleasant interactions as much as they could. This realization shocked him, for he hadn't noticed how gradually his trust in them had grown.

"Are you nervous about the wedding as well?" he asked.

"Not the wedding, exactly." Gavin let out a long breath. "The dukex has been instructing me on how to run a house. They seem to think I have a good handle on it all; I'm fairly sure I understand everything. But I...I do so want to...I don't know...do Charles proud."

Pip raised an eyebrow. "I rather think you already do."

Gavin blushed. "Thank you," he mumbled.

"So you are nervous about your older brother coming and about taking over new responsibilities?"

"Yes," Gavin said. His pace sped up slightly. Pip suspected Gavin hadn't realized it.

"Is there anything else?" he ventured.

"Well, I'm not sure if it's appropriate to discuss."

"With me?"

"With...anyone."

Pip considered. Finally, he said, "You needn't discuss it if you don't wish to, of course. But I remember you once offered to let me confess some concerns—'even if it doesn't make sense,' you said—and you didn't seem too bothered by whether or not my own concerns were appropriate. I'm happy to return the favor if you'd like."

Gavin huffed a breath. "Good point. It's...erm...well, you see, I'm a bit worried about the wedding...night."

"Oh. *Oh*," Pip said as he registered what Gavin meant. "Would you like any...I don't know...explanations?"

Gavin's blush deepened. "I couldn't possibly—I mean, with your—it would be terribly—" He broke off. "It is very kind of you. But I have no desire to make you uncomfortable."

"I can appreciate the difference between my history and your relationship," Pip said gently. "Charles loves you and he clearly respects you. It will be nothing like what I've experienced."

"I know. I just...I'm not at all sure what I'm meant to *do* and I don't wish to make a cake of myself."

"Does he expect you to have experience?"

Gavin shook his head. "Nextborns aren't supposed to have any experience before marriage."

"Then I imagine Charles will anticipate showing you what to do."

Gavin swallowed. "Yes, I suppose you're right. It's just that the long engagement has meant that my nervousness has been building up for some time. And...well, he's been waiting for all this time for my sake, and I feel foolish being nervous still."

"Considering the way he looks at you every time you enter the room, I suspect he thinks you're worth the wait."

"That would be correct," Charles said, as he walked around the bend. He gave an apologetic smile. "Sorry for overhearing, darlings. I was just coming to tell you both that dinner is ready."

Pip quickly excused himself as Charles slipped his hand around Gavin's waist.

As it turned out, Gavin was not the only person who had nerves to work out. When Pip joined Charles on an evening ride, Charles said, "I'm afraid I've been taking a longer route the past few days, darling. Do you mind?"

Pip assured him he didn't mind and they rode for a while in silence.

As they made their way back, Charles finally slowed down his pace. "I'm sorry if I exhausted you."

"I don't mind." He hesitated. "Is everything all right? You seem...nervous?"

Charles chuckled. "I suppose I am in a way, but I certainly didn't expect it."

"Why didn't you expect it?"

"Well...my parents died when I was very young, so I spent a great deal of my youth being rather lonely. Bertie helped, of course, as did Julian. I later became closer to my aunt. I haven't any siblings and precious few relatives, so I've been pining for a family. I'm surprised to be nervous when it's something I've been eagerly looking forward to for years."

"I understand that," Pip said. "I feel as though I have a similar...well, similar lack of family."

"Yes, I daresay in that way we are very much alike. Bertie is too, actually. Granted, he has a rather large extended family, but he has no siblings and his father died around the same time mine did."

"Is that—" Pip broke off, unsure if what he was going to ask was impertinent.

Charles looked at him inquiringly.

"Is that why you've taken me in? And Gerry?"

Charles smiled. "There were several reasons, but yes, that is one of them."

"You were building your own family?"

"Attempting to. Although you were a delightful surprise addition."

"Did you know who I was before I came? That I was the same person who broke into Lord Finlington's house and that I was part of that gang who—"

Charles was nodding before he'd finished the question.

"How did you trust me not to rob you?"

Charles shrugged. "It was a risk worth taking. In both of our previous encounters, I got the sense that you were a decent person, despite your occupation. You may recall, I became better acquainted with Nell, who proved herself worthy of the trust placed in her. She's always spoken very highly of you. And…" He paused. "And there's something to be said about trust going both ways. We are an easy distance from London—barely a day's ride by speed spell—but that does not mean it is easy to traverse by foot. You were trusting your own safety and happiness to a group of strangers. Considering the life you'd been living, I do not take that trust lightly. Moreover, it was…courageous to leave behind every-thing you'd known and try an entirely new career and new life. So it was more a case of matching your own courage as much as we could, giving you our trust in exchange for yours."

"Oh," Pip said quietly. He was silent for a moment and then said, "Miss Hartford—that is, Gerry—has been saying all along that I'm practically part of the family. Gavin has said it too. I…I'm still trying to understand how to be a part of this family."

Charles smiled at him. "You don't have to do anything other than what you've been doing. Have you not noticed that Gavin now looks to you for advice just as much as you look to him? You two are quite similar in many ways, you know. Gerry is much more at ease running the shop with you here than she was her first month after we moved. I can't imagine my life without you in it to some degree. And Bertie...well, Bertie is quite fond of you too, you know. You fit in our little family. I hope you stay forever."

Pip swallowed against the emotion welling inside him. "Thank you," he said quietly. Then he cleared his throat and said, "So, I suppose the Hartfords coming is not you meeting your new family, but rather our two families getting better acquainted."

Charles's grin broadened. "What a marvelous way to put it, darling."

CHAPTER 15

CHRISTMAS HAD NEVER MEANT MUCH to Pip. It sometimes meant easier marks as people were a little more carefree. Otherwise, he never had a Christmas dinner or any sort of celebration. So he was startled, and a little dismayed, when all of his friends presented him with gifts on Christmas Day. He honestly wished they hadn't. It hadn't occurred to him to buy anything for them. While he was attempting to no longer consider himself in everyone's debt, the one-sided gift exchange did not make it easier for him. This isn't to say he wasn't grateful, for he loved his gifts—new clothes from Charles, embroidered handkerchiefs enchanted with quick-dry spells from Gerry, a couple of books from Gavin, a lovely set of cravat pins from the dukex, and a walking stick from Lord Finlington. He privately decided to find gifts for his friends as soon as possible.

He enjoyed the evening celebration more. Lord Finlington and the Hearsts came to dinner, along with the Hartfords' uncle and aunt and a couple of cousins. It was Pip's first real dinner party. The large number of people intimidated him, but as he knew most of the guests, he found himself able to relax and enjoy the banter and easy conversation happening around him. After dinner, Gerry played some Christmas carols on the pianoforte, followed by a couple of her cousins, and then everyone went home.

∾

SHORTLY AFTER CHRISTMAS WAS OVER, MR. AND MRS. Hartford arrived in Tutting-on-Cress. They did not come with the dreaded older brother, much to everyone's relief. They didn't bring the younger brother either, which surprised Pip a little.

"Sebastian needs to focus on his studies," the father had explained. From what Pip gathered after listening to the Hartfords talk, Sebastian was something of a troublemaker at school and apparently a determined flirt.

"He may well ruin his reputation if he isn't sent down first," Mrs. Hartford told her daughter with a sigh. Pip couldn't entirely figure out what Sebastian had been doing that put all of his family members in grim moods. From his mental calculations, Sebastian couldn't have been more than twenty years old.

It was Pip's first time being surrounded by an actual family unit, parents and children, and he observed their interactions with interest. He concluded privately that Mr. Hartford was rather hard on his children and not particularly good at conveying his love and pride for them. The gentleman was a little gruff, of very few words, and smiled rarely—a colder and sterner version of Gavin. Mrs. Hartford was much friendlier and of softer disposition than her husband, but Pip noticed she seemed to take care not to disagree with her husband's handling of things. He thought it seemed more surprising that Gerry and Gavin had turned out to be so kind and empathetic, not rebellious or boorish like their two brothers, after what was likely a very confusing upbringing. He suspected the dukex was of a similar mind.

Anytime they were in the room, they never hesitated to contribute their opinion.

At one point, Mr. Hartford was explaining to Charles, "If Sebastian doesn't correct his behavior by the end of this term, I may well pull him from school. Although, I confess, I am unsure what to do with him."

"I suspect," the dukex said placidly from their spot across the room, "that the child needs more attention."

Mr. Hartford frowned at the dukex's words. "With all due respect, Your Grace, I rather think that boy gets more attention than is quite healthy for him."

"Not all attention is equal," Charles said, glancing at the dukex with a small smile. "Julian's had their share of taking care of troublesome children. They have very good instincts, I think."

"Thank you, Charles. I would be happy to take charge of your youngest, Mr. Hartford. I could see to it that he enters society to advantage. Some young people do not thrive in schoolrooms."

Mr. Hartford hesitated. "That is very kind of you, Your Grace. But I fear you've been spoiled by meeting my two best behaved children first. I have no desire to foist the least behaved upon you. I shall deal with Sebastian."

The dukex's lips pressed together, but they merely gave a small nod in acquiescence.

"You could always send him here," Charles said as he led Mr. Hartford out of the room. "I'm sure between Gavin, Gerry, and myself, we could straighten him out."

Mr. Hartford looked thoughtful at the suggestion and followed Charles.

"More tea, child?" the dukex said to Pip.

Pip jumped a bit at the direct question. He hadn't thought anyone had noticed he was still sitting in the room. "Yes, please." He hesitated as the dukex poured out. "You're worried about their youngest?"

The dukex sighed and passed the cup over. "In my experience, young people who act out in such a manner are doing so because they are in need of something: support, attention, empathy, patience, boundaries, freedom. There are many reasons for that child to be causing such trouble. He should have been pulled out of school ages ago."

"Sending him here might help," Pip ventured. "It helped me."

The dukex smiled warmly at him. "Yes," they said. "I would feel at ease with that solution. Between the four of you, not to mention Bertram, I'm sure young Sebastian would have everything he needed to find his own way."

"Me? You think I could help?"

The dukex poured themself a cup of tea. "Geraldine and Gavin have both mentioned the boy's friends as bad influences. I imagine having a good friend like you could go a long way. Everyone says that he doesn't take their advice. Perhaps he's slow to trust. You know a little about that."

Pip took a sip of tea and considered.

"However," the dukex continued, "if he is as big a flirt as they say, I would urge you to take care. You are still healing from your own wounds. If he does come to stay, I advise you to see to it you always have a chaperone, at least until you know him better."

"Thank you. I will. But won't you be here too?"

They shook their head. "I'll be going back to town after the wedding. I came here to act as chaperone with so many unwed people in the house. Once Charles and Gavin are married, they will be suitable chaperones themselves. Charles is, perhaps, a bit too indulgent to be a truly proper chaperone. But thankfully the countryside is more lenient."

"Oh," Pip said. "I didn't realize you would be leaving so soon."

The dukex put their teacup on the table and cupped Pip's cheek. "I'll come visit."

Pip sniffed, feeling foolish for not knowing about the dukex's departure. He had assumed their little household would stay the same. A ridiculous assumption, the more he thought about it, considering Miss Hartford had already told him she planned to get married someday.

The dukex pressed a light kiss to his forehead. "I'll miss you too, poppet."

∾

As the day of the wedding approached, everyone got a little busier. Gavin and Charles were busy preparing the house. It turned out the dukex wasn't the only one who planned to vacate the premises as soon as the wedding was over.

"We thought it would be nice to give Gavin and Charles some time alone," Gerry explained as they walked to the shop the week before the wedding. "So my parents are going to stay with my aunt and uncle before they go back to Sherton. And Julia and Rose invited you and me to stay with them at their cottage."

"Oh," Pip said. "That was kind of them."

"It will only be a fortnight," Gerry assured him. "And then we'll go back. Bertie offered his home, too. But the dukex said it wouldn't be proper for either of us to stay with him. Well, particularly you, as Bertie is of the masculine persuasion. Staying with him for a fortnight could damage your reputation."

Pip liked the Hearsts, so he wasn't exactly bothered by the idea of staying with them. But he was a trifle bothered by the notion that he wasn't permitted to stay with the viscount, even though staying with the gentleman would have intimidated him exceedingly. He was also a little startled to learn that he had a reputation that could be damaged. Hadn't his own past inflicted enough of that? Perhaps with this new life and this sham of a history that everyone gave him, he needed to play the part of a respectable gentleman.

"Lord Finlington lives quite far from the village," he said at last.

Gerry breathed out in apparent relief. "Yes," she said. "The Hearsts' cottage is much closer."

With that, the subject appeared to be resolved.

Later, however, Gerry broached the subject again as they were closing up the shop. "Do you know," she said, "that I've had the shop for almost half a year and I've never had an issue with getting supplies?"

Pip looked up from his sweeping. "Is there an issue now?"

She glanced over a shelf of jars. "My regular suppliers are telling me I'll have to go to London to get some of the things I need." She paused and seemed to be doing some sort of mental calculation. Then she stepped back and said, "You know, I think I might go to London after the wedding."

"And close the shop?" Pip said, surprised.

"Well…" she said. "You would be here. You could run it while I'm gone. Do you think you'd be comfortable running it without me?"

He didn't. "For how long?"

"A day or two. Maybe three."

"Good heavens, you know I couldn't do that," he said. "What if we ran out of spells? I have no idea how to assemble them."

"I could teach you," she said, but she didn't sound as confident as usual.

"What if I did it wrong and you weren't here to check? I would be pleased to learn how to assemble them, but I would vastly prefer it if you were here at first."

"You're right," she said. She considered. "I suppose I could ask Bertie to go for me."

"What if I went?" he asked, the idea coming to him like inspiration.

Her eyes widened. "Oh goodness, Pip. Would you?"

He supposed he ought to be anxious about the suggestion, but the more he considered it, the more he warmed to the idea. He finally had the opportunity to do something for one of his friends and he was eager to take it. Going to London was a favor he could afford. With his saved-up income, he could buy late Christmas gifts for everyone. And there was a small niggling thought at the back of his head that he might be able to find a way to pay Jack back once and for all and put his horrible past firmly behind him.

He smiled. "I would be glad to, Gerry."

"Smashing," she said. "I'll give you a list of what to buy, and the money for it, of course."

"Would you allow me to help purchase some of the materials?" he ventured.

Her smile was soft. "If you would like to, dear." She reached for his hand and gave it a gentle squeeze.

He was relieved at the prospect of being of some real use at last. Not to mention, he'd be able to delay having to stay at the Hearsts' cottage and being a burden to them, too.

That night, Lord Finlington came to dinner and Gerry explained the plan to everyone: that she was going to stay with the Hearsts for a fortnight, and Pip was going to London for a few days before staying with the Hearsts as well.

"What a clever notion," Lord Finlington said. "How lovely to have an assistant at last, eh, Gerry, darling?"

"I keep forgetting that Pip is an assistant," she said.

The viscount smiled. "More like a comrade-in-arms?"

"Precisely!"

"I wonder, Pip, if you would be so kind as to allow me to escort you on your trip?" the viscount said. "It is a long journey to take alone, especially if you are unaccustomed to it. And then we can stay in my townhouse while we are in town."

"I do not wish you to feel you must—"

"No, m'dear, I assure you. As your friend, I would like to accompany you, if you will permit."

"Of course, my lord," Pip said, feeling embarrassed by the viscount's solicitude. "I should be glad of your company."

"I will be traveling to London as well," the dukex added, looking at Lord Finlington with an unreadable expression. "So I shall be able to join you both on the way."

"Capital!" Lord Finlington said with a grin.

"And," they added to Pip, "you will be staying at *my* townhouse. I'm sure Bertram will understand."

Charles gave an unmistakable snort that he turned into a small cough. "You really do think of everything, don't you, darling?"

The dukex's smile was smug.

Pip glanced at the viscount. His enthusiasm had diminished slightly and he looked, to Pip's surprise, a little embarrassed. When he noticed Pip looking, he gave him a warm smile. Then he said to the dukex, "That will do admirably. Thank you, Your Grace."

Pip wondered if the dukex's insistence had to do with his reputation, as Gerry had mentioned earlier. He never had to worry about such things before. He privately thought the concern to be a little unnecessary. After all, he was nowhere close to the viscount's sphere. He rather thought he was more of a danger to the gentleman's reputation; not the other way around. Perhaps *that* was the issue?

He muddled over the problem for days. He still considered Lord Finlington to be one of the most attractive people he'd ever met. As he examined his own feelings, he could admit that he admired Lord Finlington, looked up to him, found him appealing, kind, intelligent, and interesting. In other circumstances, he probably would have fallen in love with the man.

As it was...well, Pip was fairly sure he'd never trust himself to fall in love. He had once believed himself to be in love with Jack, but that sentiment had soured and twisted until Pip had become disgusted with himself for even entertaining the notion. He was hardly an expert on love; it seemed best to leave romance to other people who were more capable of it.

Nevertheless, at night, he'd occasionally give in to the fantasy of the viscount seeing him as appealing in turn, much as he had entertained months ago in London. He would imagine the gentleman using a special term of endearment meant just for him, picture himself putting his head on the viscount's shoulder, think about how Lord Finlington's arms would feel around him. He thought about how sweet it would be to kiss the other man's upturned lips, how it would feel to trace the softness of his stomach, and the smoothness of his well-shaved cheeks. But since he felt sure the viscount couldn't possibly see him as anything like an equal, it still stung with the same pain of impossibility that it used to.

Two days before the wedding, everything was prepared for his trip to London. As Pip helped Jennings pack for the trip—which is to say, he flitted about trying to be helpful and mostly feeling in the way—he contemplated what it would be like to return to London. So much had changed about his circumstances since he had left. He knew himself to have changed as well.

He was both excited and nervous about the prospect of visiting the city that had been his only home for so long, where he had first felt fear and misery. He worried a little that the viscount's offer to join him was partially out of distrust or fear that Pip would run away. He tried to comfort himself from that niggling worry by thinking instead that it may have been more out of concern for Pip's safety and comfort. This both cheered him and made him feel guilty.

The night before the wedding, Pip decided he was relieved that the dukex had intervened. He felt sure that if he stayed in the viscount's house overnight, he would be horribly distracted by the knowledge that Lord Finlington was sleeping nearby. Pip had a notion that the viscount would be a very enjoyable person to curl up next to, for he suspected the man would be as tender and kind in action as he was in word. The notion sparked a strange and gentle yearning to slip into the gentleman's bed and snuggle under the covers with him. Naturally, after imagining that, it took forever for him to fall asleep. His mind was a tumultuous mess of thoughts and worries. It was well into the morning when he finally dozed off.

The day of the wedding, he was relieved by the small assembly, especially as it was all people he knew. Gerry sat next to him and took his hand in hers as she watched, dabbing her eyes a little with a handkerchief. Pip looked about him and realized that everyone was either family or very close friends. The fact that he was considered a close enough friend to be present made him want to cry too.

When Charles spoke his vows, Gavin looked at him as though he could hardly believe he was real. When Gavin spoke his vows in return, Charles pulled the other man into an embrace and passionate kiss, in what Pip suspected was a breach in proper protocol, if the dukex's tutting was anything to go by. Pip glanced at the dukex and was relieved to note that they weren't really annoyed, merely exasperated in a fond sort of way. Pip turned back to the couple and couldn't help but grin when they broke off the kiss and Gavin's face lit up with a rare smile.

Afterwards, the couple walked home, followed by a crowd of villagers who had come to cheer them on. Pip and the others followed in the newlyweds' wake, and he allowed the crowd to buoy his spirits rather than intimidate him. He was, after all, surrounded by his family.

Once they returned home, there was a large and sumptuous meal. Gavin seemed particularly on edge throughout the event. When someone suggested leaving the newlyweds alone and Gavin blushed under the subsequent attention, Pip remembered their conversation in the garden and realized the young man was anxious about the intimacy that was to come. He relaxed a little at the realization, feeling confident in Charles's ability to calm Gavin's nerves.

After breakfast, Pip's belongings and the dukex's trunks were loaded onto a carriage. Lord Finlington's carriage was then brought forward. He helped Pip inside, the dukex sat beside him, and the viscount sat on the seat opposite, much as he had on their journey there. The viscount informed him that they would place the speed spell as soon as they reached the country road.

This time, the viscount did not prompt Pip as he placed the materials on the road—although he did need assistance with the sigil. The viscount had him do the incantation, repeating it until Pip had it right. Pip employed his recent studies of feeling magic to sense when the spell had taken hold and he kept those senses up as he took the preparations apart. He could feel the spell still attached to the carriage and the horses, but as he rubbed the sigil out of the dirt, he felt the last traces of the spell on the road melt away.

"Marvelous job," the viscount said as Pip stood. "My word, darling, you do have the knack."

Cheered by his success, Pip climbed back into the carriage. It was strange, traveling on the power of his own spell, with a book in hand, and returning to London a different man than when he had left it. He found himself looking out the window, his book lying open in his hands, lost in thought.

"All right, m'dear?" Lord Finlington said.

Pip started and then smiled at the gentleman. "Yes, sir. Just thinking how different it is to be going...back."

"Not a bad feeling, I hope?" the dukex said.

"No," Pip said. "A good one. I feel as if I'm a different person now. I feel as though I shall find London a different place than when I left it."

The dukex returned his smile. "I daresay you will."

When they stopped to recast the speed spell twenty-five miles later, Pip managed entirely by himself with no prompts, reminders, or assistance. He felt the magic for balance, looked up at the viscount for assurance, and then cast the spell.

He felt inordinately pleased with himself as he climbed into the carriage. It seemed to him that he had passed an unspoken test by re-casting the very first spell he ever attempted. He thought about how it would feel when he paid off his debt with Jack, another test he had yet to pass. His stomach churned with nerves at the prospect of encountering Jack, but he was determined. Lord Finlington had once said that he was responsible for overseeing Pip's redemption, and Pip was determined to prove himself worthy.

CHAPTER 16

THEY REACHED LONDON BY NIGHTFALL. Pip was awed upon entering the dukex's palatial townhouse. It looked at least twice as large as Lord Finlington's London home. Inside, the house gleamed with white marble and alabaster stone. He felt exceedingly out of place among the grandeur.

As usual, his friends treated him as if he belonged. The dukex had him shown to a beautiful room overlooking the street. They all ate dinner together, which made Pip a trifle nervous. Both the dukex and the viscount made an evident effort to put Pip at ease, but he found himself unnerved by their focused attention. He was constantly tripping over his own tongue in responding to the viscount's polite inquiries. Pip slept fitfully, being in a strange house with strange surroundings.

After breakfast the next morning, Lord Finlington returned to invite Pip for a ride in the park. "Charlie tells me you have an excellent seat, darling."

Pip felt his face flush. The viscount chuckled. "I mean to say, my sweet, that you are an excellent horseman."

"Oh," Pip said, breathing out in relief. "Thank you, sir. I daresay he has given me far more credit than I deserve."

"I highly doubt that," the viscount said with a smile. "But, in any case, you will find riding in London to be a far tamer affair than the country."

"I should love to, sir, but I do need to shop for Gerry's spell materials." He did not add that he planned to visit Jack's tavern, too.

The dukex interceded, saying, "Plenty of time for that tomorrow, poppet. We both thought it would be nice for you to relax today."

"In that case, I would be honored to go to the park with you."

To Pip's surprise, the dukex did not insist on joining. After extracting a promise from the viscount that he would return Pip in an hour, they seemed satisfied and instructed Pip to enjoy himself.

What Lord Finlington failed to mention was that riding in Hyde Park was really a way for people to meet and chat. Pip discovered this when they reached the park and he was mildly horrified to see how many people were there.

"Have you never been to Hyde Park, darling?" the viscount said, clearly amused by Pip's shock.

"I confess, I always gave the horses a wide berth, sir," Pip responded. "As such I did not realize how many of them there were."

The viscount chuckled. "Come along then, darling. And don't fret. I shall introduce you as a friend from Tutting-on-Cress. No one shall ask the particulars."

This proved to be true, although the viscount made the introduction to many more people than Pip would have thought possible in a one-hour period. Everyone seemed very polite and pleased to know him, and Pip detected no small amount of curiosity in many of their expressions at meeting him by way of Lord Finlington. He wondered if people would assume they were together and the prospect both unnerved and pleased him.

They returned to the dukex's townhouse for lunch and the

viscount announced that he had planned an outing for all three of them to the theater.

"I hazard a guess that you have never been to the opera, m'dear," he said. "I thought it might be an enjoyable experience for you. And we can visit dear Nell."

Pip smiled at him. "That was very thoughtful of you, sir. I would like that."

"Splendid!" the viscount said. Pip thought he looked relieved.

Dressing for the opera required much more elegance than Pip was prepared for. The dukex instructed a servant to dress Pip in one of the outfits Charles had gifted him for Christmas, one that included a brocade waistcoat. Pip had wondered when he'd received it where he might have occasion to wear such finery. He supposed the opera was one such occasion. The dukex met him downstairs wearing a satin turban that matched their cravat pin and looking incredibly elegant. Lord Finlington arrived in similarly stunning finery and took them in his carriage to the opera.

Pip kept hoping he would be able to approach the opera house with outer calm, but when he stepped out and saw Covent Garden, he felt as if all of the blood had rushed out of his head. The viscount caught him under the arm.

"All right, darling?" he said.

Pip was grateful no one was out front yet. Perhaps tonight wasn't the night for the market. He hoped so. "Yes, I'm all right. Sorry."

The dukex studied him for a long moment. "Would you prefer to go home?" they asked.

Pip considered saying yes, but he hated the idea of Nell looking forward to their visit and missing him. So he took a deep breath and shook his head.

Lord Finlington offered Pip his arm, and though he felt shy taking it, he was grateful to have the viscount beside him as they went inside. He had never been through the front of the theater before, only the backstage area to visit Nell when she first got her job. He stared at the velvet curtains and the marble pillars, distracted by the finery of the other theatergoers, and pretended that it was an entirely different place, and that he himself had never been offered up to its patrons.

When the curtains went up and the opera began, Pip was completely enthralled by the performance. It affected him like Gavin's poetry books, or Gerry playing the pianoforte, the music lilting over him like an evening breeze. He allowed himself to be swept up by the feeling.

When it was over, he wasted no time in turning to the viscount and thanking him. "I've never heard anything so wonderful," he said.

The viscount beamed at him. "I'm so glad, darling."

Lord Finlington then led the way through the crowd, but instead of going back outside, they went toward the stage. He paid an usher to let them through a side door to the backstage area. Pip recognized the smell of the wood, the sight of the sandbags holding down the ropes, and the jostling of the people as they moved around backstage.

Then he heard someone say, "Pip!" and found himself engulfed in a hug. As soon as he realized it was Nell, he hugged her back.

She pulled away and grinned at him. "My goodness, it's good to see you!" she said. She gave him a small once-over. "You look different."

He shrugged a little. "I suppose I am a bit different."

She laughed. "In a good way, I hope."

He smiled. "Yes. Definitely in a good way."

She hugged him again and then turned to greet the viscount and the dukex. Pip noticed that Nell seemed a little unsure of how to greet the dukex. Finally, she turned back to Bertie and said, "I want you to meet my friends."

To his surprise, she led them onto the stage, where she introduced a young woman named Betsy and another person named Mx. Harriet. They looked vaguely familiar, and Pip recalled having met them the one time he came to visit Nell while he was still living in London.

"Betsy trained me," Nell explained. "And Harriet helps with the scenery."

Harriet flicked a long braid over their shoulder. "I'm much more important than she makes it sound."

"We met you when you came to visit before, didn't we?" Betsy said to Pip, ignoring Harriet's comment. "Aren't you the one who went to the country?" Pip nodded. "Good. I'm glad to see you're all right. She was a wreck after you were arrested," she added.

Pip glanced at Nell. Had she told everyone about that?

Harriet looked at Pip thoughtfully. "You know," they said. "He's as pretty as Lino."

He blinked at them. "You know Lino?"

Their eyes widened. "*You* know Lino?"

"Who doesn't know him?" Betsy said with a laugh. "He's here tonight. You might catch him on your way out if you keep an eye skinned."

Pip felt his mouth go dry at her words. "He is?" He supposed he shouldn't have been all that surprised to learn that some of the other theater people knew Lino; after all, he'd talked to Lino inside the theater shortly after Nell had started working there. It was probably only months ago, though it felt like a lifetime had passed. But he'd hoped the foyer would be empty that night. Would Jack be out there?

Nell grabbed his arm. "Can I talk to you for a moment?" she said.

Still grappling with the realization that he'd have to exit through the crowd outside the theater, he allowed her to lead him away from the little group.

She did not seem concerned with whether the viscount and the dukex would be properly entertained by Betsy and

Harriet. She pulled him to a corner and said in a hushed tone, "Pip, I...I need to tell you..."

"What?" he said, matching her tone, feeling alarmed.

She took a deep breath. "I didn't know. And I'm so sorry."

"Didn't know?"

"About Jack. I didn't know what he did to you."

He took a moment to process her words. "How do you know now?"

"Lino told me."

Pip wasn't surprised to hear that. Lino was certainly in a position to know about Pip's sordid history. He'd been present most nights when Jack took Pip to Covent Garden.

"I...I wish you'd been able to tell me," she continued. "But I know why you didn't. I'm sorry I wasn't...I wasn't what you needed me to be."

He blinked at her. "You were exactly what I needed you to be."

"No," she said, with a sad smile. "If I had been, I would have seen how miserable you were and I would have been able to get you out."

Pip chewed on his lip. "I think the only way I could have gotten out was to leave town. We both know I couldn't have done that, not really, without someone like Lord Finlington to help."

She sighed. "I suppose. All the same—"

"It's fine, Nelly," he said. "You didn't know. I didn't tell you. I'm sorry that I...couldn't. But thank you for getting me out of prison. I would still be there if you hadn't told his lordship."

She smiled and gave him another tight hug. "I didn't realize helping you meant you would go so far away. But you seem much better now."

"I am."

"Good," she said as she pulled away. "You know, you never responded to my letter."

He ducked his head. "Sorry. When I received it, I couldn't read yet. And then I…um…forgot."

"Hm," she said, in a tone that suggested she didn't believe him in the slightest. Which was fair, since it was a complete falsehood.

"Did you ever tell Jack that I—"

"No," she said quickly. "I didn't tell him anything."

He sighed in relief. "Thank you." He glanced over his shoulder. "I probably shouldn't keep the dukex or his lord-ship waiting."

She cocked her head and looked at him. "Why don't you call him Bertie?"

He shrugged and looked at the ground. "I don't think I've earned that yet."

"You know he'd love it if you did."

He didn't reply as they walked back to the little group.

"Are you ready to leave, m'dear?" the viscount said. Pip nodded. "It was lovely to see you again, darling," Lord Finlington said to Nell.

"Thank you for visiting!" she said. "I told Pip he should call you Bertie."

Pip wanted to elbow her but was surprised to see the viscount blush a little.

"Well," he said. "It's no matter, my sweet. I'm not sure I've earned that yet."

"That's what Pip said," she added. Pip considered step-ping on her foot. Lord Finlington chuckled.

The dukex swept forward and put an arm around Pip's shoulders. "I think it's time we went home. Lovely to see you all. Thank you for your hospitality, Miss Birks. Come along, Bertram. The carriage will have been brought around by now."

They strode out of the theater, with Pip under their arm, and the viscount in their wake. But when Pip stepped into the foyer, he felt as if he might faint. The sight of the vendors and the harlots was all too familiar.

The dukex's arm tightened around his shoulder. "I've got you, poppet," they said quietly. "It's all right."

It took all his energy to keep up with the dukex's hurried steps. For a moment, he wondered if Lino really was there and if he'd see and recognize Pip. The thought filled him with embarrassment until he remembered that Lino, of all people, would likely understand.

Finally, they reached the street where the viscount's carriage was waiting. The dukex pulled him so his head rested on their shoulder and he allowed himself to curl in slightly in the comfort of their embrace.

"Oh, m'dear," the viscount said as the carriage moved down the street. "Are you all right?"

"He used to bring me here to...to offer me up," Pip said quietly.

"Oh, darling," the viscount whispered. "I am sorry. If I had known—"

"It's all right," Pip said hurriedly. Then, after a moment's hesitation, he reached out a hand and was relieved when the viscount took it. "I loved the opera. And thank you for taking me to see Nell. That was so kind of you."

Lord Finlington squeezed his hand. Pip relaxed against the dukex's shoulder and barely noticed the journey to the townhouse and to his bed.

CHAPTER 17

THE NEXT MORNING, Pip woke up later than usual, and made his way to the large breakfast room. The dukex looked up at his entrance with evident concern. "Are you all right, child?"

"I'm sorry about—"

They held up a hand. "No need to apologize, poppet. We would not have taken you if we had known."

"I know." He walked to the sideboard and filled up his plate. "I'm glad I went, though," he said as he sat down.

They patted his hand. "Well, you are welcome to stay here as long as you wish. So if you need to delay the shopping until tomorrow when you're more recovered—"

Pip shook his head. "Thank you," he added hastily when he realized he'd interrupted them. "I'd like to do that today. It will be good to—" He broke off and felt his face flush.

They tilted their head and waited for him to continue.

"It will be good to do something useful for Gerry, after everything she's done for me."

They gave him a warm smile and squeezed his hand. "Very good, child. Bertram will be here soon to ensure you know where to go. I trust you have a list of things to purchase?"

He nodded and pulled a piece of paper out of his pocket.

"Excellent. Eat your breakfast now. The shopping can wait."

Pip originally planned to go see Jack before he went shopping. After the shock of the previous night, he considered asking to delay his return to Tutting-on-Cress in order to go visit Jack the following morning. He was relieved by the dukex's open invitation to stay in London longer. Once he purchased what Gerry needed, he would gather up the courage to settle his debts. Thus encouraged, he ate his breakfast and waited for Lord Finlington.

When the viscount arrived a half hour later, Pip presented him with his shopping list.

"Wonderful," he said. "I drew up a list of what I thought you might need. It looks as though I made a pretty good guess." He pulled out a pencil and a slip of paper from his own pocket and crossed a few things out. "There," he said. "Now they're a match. I've taken the liberty of writing how much each item should cost, taking into account any shortages or droughts. If a spellmaster charges you higher than this, they are cheating you. Refuse their price until they offer something reasonable."

Pip took the paper, studying the prices listed. The viscount pointed to the bottom of the paper. "Here are the shops in London that sell magical materials. I have listed them with their addresses in order from most respectable to least. I should tell you that Smelting is a mean old swindler, but he does often have the hard-to-get items."

Pip had not realized the task would be so involved. However, he felt as though this was another great test to undertake. Everyone was placing a great deal of trust in him. Pip had no intention whatsoever of giving up his life in Tutting-on-Cress; he had found real happiness for the first time and he was in no desire to lose it. But none of his new friends knew this with certainty, so he was a little awed by their faith in him.

"Thank you, my lord," he said. He hesitated and said, "I want you both to know I'm aware of the trust you're placing in me for this task. I swear I shall come back as soon as possible."

The dukex smiled at him. "We had no doubt of it, poppet."

"Do you wish to have company?" the viscount offered.

Pip stammered that the viscount was most welcome to join, but he could manage alone.

"Very good," Lord Finlington replied. "I'm sure wandering through London will be a unique experience and you may wish for solitude. However, I hope you will permit me to insist on some precautionary measures."

He pulled a small bag from his coat pocket and handed it to Pip. "This is a protection spell," he said. "It will give the user a temporary, invisible bubble, as it were, of protection. However, it is very short-lived, so I advise you to hold off on using it until you feel you may be in danger. Although brief, it is powerful and very easy to activate. I have put all of the ingredients into a fine powder. All you have to do is sprinkle a bit of the powder over your person and say the incantation." He told Pip the incantation, having him repeat until he had it right, as he had done the previous day with the travel spell. "Very good," he said. "Keep it handy. I hope you won't have to use it."

Pip was tolerably confident he wouldn't, but he accepted the bag gratefully.

"Before you go, I do hate to ask, darling, but do you have enough money to get all of the ingredients?"

Pip told him how much he had and the viscount nodded, satisfied. "Very good," he said. "If you struggle to find anything, I'll be happy to return to the shops with you this afternoon or tomorrow."

Pip thanked him and donned his things to leave the house. Standing on the stoop, he placed his purse in a pocket that he knew was the most difficult to reach. The spell bag would feel like a purse to a pickpocket, so he stashed it in the same place. He would have preferred to keep it more easily accessible, but decided he would have to trust his own intuition to pull the bag out quickly enough. Even if he was held up by thieves, he could pull out the bag as if to hand it over and dump the contents onto himself at that point. Assured, he strode down the street.

Starting at the top of the viscount's list, he went to the first shop listed. He was relieved when they had several of the items he needed at a decent price. The second shop provided almost all of the rest. But the third and fourth shops did not have the final ingredient he needed. The spellmaster at the third shop assured Pip that it was rare, for it was dangerous to acquire. Pip made his way to Smelting's.

Throughout his shopping trip, he recognized the jostled bumps and tiny bits of pressure near his pockets. But at every shop, he had checked that his purse and the spell bag were still in place. It was strange to walk down narrow streets that had once felt like home, and stranger still to be seen as a mark and not a fellow thief.

Pip carefully did not make eye contact for fear of being recognized. Within two blocks of the last spell shop, he became aware that he had gained a shadow. It was an unsettling discovery, but he reasoned himself out of being too anxious, considering he had the protection spell. He reached Smelting's with no mishaps. Mr. Smelting did not recognize him and, as the viscount predicted, had the rare ingredient. He also attempted to sell it at three times its worth. Pip had a hard job of talking the man down, but he succeeded.

Once he paid for everything, he replaced his purse and briefly considered pulling out his spell. But he wasn't certain he would have difficulty. After all, whoever was tailing him might recognize him. He wasn't sure if this would help or hinder him, but his intuition told him that his former cohorts would be less apt to kill him immediately. Besides, he was worried he might use up the spell before he lost the thieves shadowing him.

Resolving to stick with his previously made plan, he left the spell nestled in his pocket beside his purse. Then, he hefted his packages so they were primarily resting on one arm, but looked like they were supported by both. If he had learned anything as a pickpocket, it was that being underestimated could be used to advantage.

They were waiting for him: Davey Smith, Jimmy Connor, Tommy Connor, and Bill Stark. Pip was struck by the bizarre parallel to when he had first encountered Charles. They looked surprised when he walked out; he suspected they had not yet managed to fully see his face. There was a moment of silent shock and then they all began talking at once.

"Well blow me down, if it ain't Pip!"

"We heard you were in prison!"

"How'd you get out?"

"How'd you get them fancy duds?"

Davey waved them all into silence. "What is all this?" he asked, more from curiosity, Pip thought, than anger.

Pip shrugged. "I was let out of prison. I've been living in the country. Only came back to town to do a bit of shopping for my employer."

"Does Jack know you're here?" Jimmy said.

Pip shook his head. "I only just arrived."

"He'll want to see you," Jimmy said.

Pip wasn't sure if he was ready to face Jack yet, and he wasn't fond of the idea of carrying his purchases all the way across town. "I really should get back."

"And have Jack skin us alive for not bringing you to see him?" Davey said. "Not likely."

Pip considered. Much as it annoyed him to have his carefully made plans disrupted, going immediately to Jack would allow him to take care of his debt sooner rather than later.

Besides, he still had the protection spell Lord Finlington had given him. It was probably better to see Jack while he was armed with that, and he couldn't very well ask for another without admitting to his plan.

Finally, he said, "All right."

As he was escorted back to the tavern, the other men crowded him, asking him all sorts of questions: What had he been doing all this time? Where was he living? Who had sprung him from prison? Had he thrown over Jack for someone else?

He was relieved that they weren't resentful of his change in status and amused that they would occasionally bump into him in such a way that he was sure they were searching his pockets. They were not angry with him; but he was now considered fair game.

CHAPTER 18

His escorts took him all the way into the tavern and right up to Jack. Pip wasn't surprised; Davey was always angling for a way to get into the man's good graces.

"Look what we found strolling through the streets, Jack!" Davey shouted, before shoving Pip forward.

Jack caught him by the shoulders and stared, his eyes wide. "Bless my soul," he whispered. Then he pulled Pip into a tight embrace. The packages Pip was holding buffered him against the impact, but Jack quickly remedied that, flinging the whole bundle onto the nearby table. "Pip," he said into Pip's hair. "My Pip. You've come back. I took you for lost, boy."

Pip's hat tumbled off his head and he felt crushed by the memories the embrace piled onto him. Panic started to build in his chest. Nothing had changed. Jack hadn't changed; his ginger hair, his broad shoulders, the chin rough with speckled hairs, those beautiful blue eyes framed by light-colored lashes. He still smelled the same (what Pip now realized was a disgusting mixture of ale, sweat, grime, and the stale scent of sex), his big arms around Pip felt the same, those hands already caressing his hair and body felt exactly the same. He trembled with the weight of it all and cursed himself for his own weakness. He immediately realized it was a mistake to have come, but he couldn't reach the bag while Jack gripped him to his chest.

"Did you see his new duds, Jack?" one of the men behind him said. "Don't he look a picture?"

Jack pulled back and gave Pip a quick once over. "My, my," he said, stroking Pip's cheek. "That you do."

Before he had time to react, Jack had Pip's cloak undone and one of the boys swiped it off his shoulders. He idly wondered how much Jack would get for it, as he knew he would never see that garment again. Then he realized Jack's nimble fingers were unhooking his coat buttons and he couldn't even protest before Jack had those undone too. His walking stick was snatched swiftly out of his grip. Then the coat was off. He was not prepared to be stripped by Jack in the middle of the tavern, so he held up his hands to forestall the unbuttoning of his waistcoat, which Jack looked on the verge of doing. Jack took hold of both of Pip's wrists with one large hand and slowly slid the gloves off Pip's hands, his smile sly. It was a move Pip had fantasized Lord Finlington doing, only in his dreams the action had seemed like it would be tender and intimate. He was saddened by the destruction of that fantasy.

"Jack, please. I just came to—"

Jack cut him off with a kiss, heated and demanding, and all too familiar.

Dazedly, he realized Jack was pulling him down to perch on his lap in exactly the way Jack always favored. Only this time, Jack twisted in the seat so Pip was wedged between him and the table. One of Pip's arms was trapped at his side and he was irritated to have been caught so off guard as to let it happen. Even worse, Jack reached into the pocket of his waistcoat and, with a tug, pulled out the purse, which he dumped unceremoniously onto the table, and the protection spell.

"What's this?" Jack asked, sniffing it.

"Powder, for my employer," Pip lied.

Jack raised an eyebrow and tossed it out of arm's reach. Next, he undid Pip's cravat, sliding it off Pip's neck with relish. Then he rested one hand on Pip's thigh and his other hand began the old habit of stroking through Pip's hair. It was all so horrifyingly familiar.

Jack leaned forward and began kissing Pip's temple, his jaw, his neck. "God, you taste delicious. Even better than you used to."

Pip swallowed. "Jack, I'm not here to come back. I came here to pay off my debts to you."

Jack laughed softly into Pip's cheek. "That's not our way, boy."

"How much, Jack?"

Jack tilted Pip's head so he could begin kissing the underside of his jaw. "Who sprung you from prison?"

"A stranger."

Jack nipped Pip's ear. "There's no one in London who's met you and is a stranger to me. Out with it, boy."

Pip sighed. "The gentleman from the Fox & Thistle."

Jack hummed thoughtfully and Pip felt the vibration against his skin. "Thought that one wanted a taste of you. Guess he finally got it, eh?"

"No, Jack. It's not like that. He hasn't tried anything."

"Really?" He seemed pleased. "That is surprising."

"How much do I owe you? Just tell me how much and I'll pay it off, all of it, whatever it is."

The fingers resting on his thigh began to stroke gently. "I rather like these new trousers," Jack said thoughtfully. "I think I'll have you keep those."

"How much, Jack? Please?"

The hands on his thigh moved upward and Jack pressed a bruising kiss to Pip's neck. "Now, you know that isn't our way," he said again. "I'll take payment from you the same as I always have."

Pip gasped as Jack's fingers stroked along the center seam of his trousers.

"I'm not paying that way anymore, Jack. I'll pay you with money this time or nothing." And then, boldly, "Name your price. Any amount you say."

He knew it to be a dangerous promise to make to such a man. After all, he only had so much money on him. But Pip was getting desperate and he impulsively decided that he would rather get help from Lord Finlington and feel guilty and ashamed from being indebted to the viscount than stay a moment longer on Jack's lap.

Jack's lips were grazing across Pip's cheek. "You've changed," he said.

"Yes," Pip whispered. "That happens sometimes."

"After all I did for you."

"I'll pay you back for all that."

"No," he said, pulling back a little and tilting Pip's head to look him in the face. "You know you owe me more than money."

"No," Pip responded softly. "I don't think I do. Name your price, Jack."

"You heard my price," he said, his fingers stroking Pip's trouser seam.

"Money," Pip repeated, his voice strained. "Good God, Jack. I'm telling you to name your price and you can't even give me one?"

Jack stared at him for a long, hard moment. His fingers, which Pip remembered to always be in motion, were petting Pip's throat while he thought. "You know," he said. "I used to say that you and Nell were alike in a way the rest of us weren't."

Distracted by the abrupt change in topic, Pip said, "What do you mean?"

Jack looked pensive. "You both fight for people and principles first. Money always comes last for you." He grinned. "It's probably why you're so bad at negotiating."

"He's only saying that because he doesn't understand it," said a new voice from behind.

One of the last people Pip ever expected to see in Jack's tavern, Lino Bowles walked into view and plopped himself on the bench next to Jack. Lino was still as strikingly attractive as Pip remembered him, with light brown skin, a dark curly mop of hair, freckles dotting his cheeks, and long lashes framing his dark eyes. However, Pip recalled that the young man had always seemed almost carefree in manner. Now, there was a tightness to his expression that felt both out of place on his handsome face but also dreadfully familiar.

"Well, Pip," he said with a forced smile. "Didn't think I'd ever see you again. And certainly never here."

"I was thinking the same thing," Pip said slowly.

Jack kissed Pip's cheek. "Someone was late getting out of bed."

Lino rolled his eyes.

"You're with Jack now?" Pip said, unable to keep the horror out of his voice. It felt like a lifetime ago that Lino had offered to help him with his Jack problems. Lino had been the only person to recognize Pip's misery. Pip couldn't rectify that past conversation with the idea of Lino in Jack's control.

Jack chuckled. "Jealous, Pip?"

Pip didn't answer, waiting instead for Lino to respond. Lino's smile softened. "No," he said. "He's just a customer. No need to fret about me."

Pip relaxed a little at the words. Unfortunately, Jack took that as a cue to resume his stroking. Pip immediately tensed again.

To his surprise, Lino reached forward and took Jack's hand between his own. "Jack," he said. "Why can't you let him go?"

Jack smirked, tightened his grip on Lino's hand, and then tugged the younger man forward. Then he reached up to cup Lino's chin and rubbed his thumb across Lino's lips. "Such a pretty mouth. It's a pity you haven't yet learned when no one wants to hear from it."

"You forget," Lino said, "that I don't belong to you."

"How many times must I tell you, boy," Jack said, pulling on Lino's chin to bring him closer, "that when I set my mind on someone, I always get them."

"Pip got away."

"And now he's right back where he belongs."

"I'm not staying," Pip said. "And whatever Lino owes you, I'll pay that too."

"I owe him nothing," Lino said. "I've been very careful about that."

Jack laughed. "I think that's enough of your lip, boy. Davey," he said, raising his voice. "Keep him quiet, will you?"

Davey stepped forward and yanked Lino off the bench, pinning his arms behind his back. Lino tried to pull away, but Davey was bigger and stronger. His hands gripped Lino's arms with what looked like painful tightness.

Lino raised his chin, looking stubborn. "You really think this is a good idea, Jack? How will it look to all of your loyal subjects when they find out that you're holding me against my will? Particularly when I haven't taken you up on any of your so-called generosity?"

Davey snorted. "You think anyone will care what happens to you, little harlot?"

Lino's expression looked pained for a moment, but he made a brave attempt to hide it.

Jack sighed. "I thought I told you to keep him quiet."

Jimmy laughed and clapped his hand over Lino's mouth.

Pip tilted his head down and looked up at Jack through his eyelashes, just as Jack had taught him to do. "You might keep me here by force, but you know you'll never have all of me. You'll never have my heart or soul like you used to. Why bother? I can pay you enough to go find another boy who will love you with everything he has. Let us go, Jack. You don't need us."

Jack chuckled and skimmed his hand up Pip's leg again. "You're a bit out of practice, aren't you?"

Jimmy made a disgusted noise and pulled his hand away from Lino's mouth. "He licked me," he said.

"Just reminding you," Lino said, looking satisfied with himself, "that Pip is not alone anymore. He has friends. Rich, powerful ones. You really think they'll let him be snatched like this? They'll come looking."

"I've heard that before," Davey said.

Jimmy went to cover Lino's mouth again and then hesitated. Jack snatched Pip's discarded cravat and held it up. Jimmy grinned and grabbed it, tying it around Lino's mouth in a gag.

"That's better," Jack said. "He's still learning to heel yet. Taking him longer than it took you."

"That's because he's a great deal smarter than I was," Pip said. "You'll never hold him. Just like you could never hold Nell."

Jack rolled his eyes. "Nell was useless."

"Nell was one of the cleverest people you had," Pip countered. "She knew she could do better than be a thief. She knew she could do better than this life. She didn't need you." He paused, looking at Jack thoughtfully. "And you knew that. That's why you let her go. I wonder why you don't see that Lino doesn't need you anymore than Nell did. I don't either. We'll both fight you with everything we have until we're dead or we're gone." He allowed for a small, coy smile. "I think we'd both be worth more to you if you were paid now than if we fought you to our graves."

"Oh, I don't know," Jack said, looking amused. "I think I'd get a great deal of pleasure out of both of you first."

"Name your price, Jack," Pip said. "I'll pay you double whatever I owe you, if you let us both go."

Jack hummed thoughtfully and nuzzled Pip's neck. "Double, eh? As it so happens," he said, his voice dangerously quiet, "I do have a figure in mind. Do you remember when your gentleman friend told me that what I'd been offered to steal that quizzing glass of his was a—what did he call it? Oh, yes, 'a paltry sum?'"

Pip was confused by another seemingly abrupt change in topic. "Yes."

"Well, I did some looking into the matter. Turns out, what your toff paid me was also a paltry sum. A fraction of what the item is worth."

Pip huffed. "It does belong to him, after all."

It was a foolish thing to say, and Pip regretted the words as soon as they were out of his mouth. The hand on his throat tightened and the expression in Jack's eyes went cold.

"Nobody cheats me, boy. So," he continued, his tone light again, "you get me that quizzing glass and we'll call it even."

Pip gaped. "You must be joking."

Jack smirked. "The way I see it, you've got several choices before you. You can both agree to behave yourselves, and I'll take care of you like I always did. We could have a lot of fun, the three of us."

"You said several choices," Pip said.

"Or if you want me all to yourself like before, Lino can agree to work in one of my harlot houses."

"Definitely not."

"Or," Jack went on, "you can steal that quizzing glass for me and I'll let you both go. You know I pride myself on being fair, Pip. And that's more than fair."

Jack had trapped him and they both knew it. No matter what option Pip picked, he would lose the friendship and trust of all the people he had come to know and love in Tutting-on-Cress. Jack was neatly taking away his future with the same dexterity with which he had stolen away his past.

"Now," he said, kissing Pip's temple. "What'll it be?"

Pip knew his decision before he said the words and he hated himself for it. "The quizzing glass."

Jack turned Pip's head and kissed him hard on the mouth. Then pulled away and grinned. "I'll miss you, Pip. You always were my favorite."

If he weren't so frightened, Pip would have rolled his eyes. He had heard Jack say those words, or something similar, to practically everybody.

Then he was yanked to stand. As soon as his feet hit the floor, he realized his shoes had been pulled off. He hadn't even noticed. He grimaced at the prospect of trudging across London in stockinged feet in January but, frankly, it was the least of his problems.

While he was realizing all of this, Jack relieved him of his waistcoat, keeping one hand firmly around the back of Pip's neck.

"It's a shame you don't have any bits and bobs on you," Jack said, sliding a hand down Pip's torso. He slid the hand back up and cupped Pip's cheek. "It didn't have to be this way, you know."

Jack wrapped his arm around Pip's shoulders, tugging him close. "Davey. Jimmy," he said. "You're coming too. Bring Lino with you." He gripped Lino's chin again. "Since the foolish boy is so intent on involving himself. You got anything to make sure he behaves? Make sure they both behave, really."

Jimmy grinned, pulled out a knife, and held it up to Lino's throat.

"Lovely," Jack said. He kissed Lino's temple. "Come along."

Pip stumbled along in Jack's grip. It was a long, cold, miserable, and painful trek across London.

CHAPTER 19

DUSK HAD STARTED to settle by the time they reached the townhouse. He wondered if the viscount was home or if he was waiting for Pip to return to the dukex's townhouse. He couldn't decide which answer would be worse.

His stockings were shredded, his feet were bleeding and bruised, and he was shivering under Jack's arm. He hated how much he needed the warmth of the man.

Jimmy got the back window open for them. Jack slipped through the window first, and Jimmy scooped Pip up and dumped him through and into Jack's arms. Jack gestured at the others to stay behind, then regained his grip on the back of Pip's neck and as he pulled a knife out of his own pocket. Pip had never seen Jack with a knife before. He hadn't realized he could be any more frightened of the man than he already was.

When they reached the study, Jack switched up his grip from Pip's neck to his hair, shoving him down to his knees and coming to stand over him, his legs bracketing Pip in place. Without a word, he passed Pip a lock pick and Pip got to work.

Now that he had some training in magic, Pip was able to sense what he hadn't the first time. He could feel the spell blocking the lock and he could feel the way the magic nudged and squirmed against the lock pick. As he worked, Jack maneuvered the knife in his hand so that he could stroke Pip's cheek. With his heightened sense of awareness of magic, and the added initiative to get Jack to stop petting him, Pip picked the lock faster than he would have thought possible.

"Nicely done," Jack whispered. He tipped Pip's chin up and kissed him on the forehead. "Very nicely done, my boy. Glad to see some of what I taught you stuck. Now, open the door."

Pip did as he was told, feeling the tug of Lord Finlington's trap spell pulling at him like a magnet as soon as the door swung open. The room was completely dark, as if it were the middle of the night and not the early evening. He wondered vaguely if that was more magic or if he had taken longer to undo the lock than he'd thought.

Hauling him up by his hair, Jack yanked Pip to his feet, and swiftly moved the knife around to settle at his throat. Pip recognized the cue and stepped forward into the study.

No sooner had they both reached the closest of the wing-back chairs, light filled the room, on the candles and in the fireplace. The door behind them snapped shut. Seated on the edge of the desk, with his legs crossed, was Lord Finlington.

"Pip, darling," he said jovially. "How delightful to see you. I take it the shopping trip did not go as planned?"

Pip was feeling conflicting emotions of hope and dismay at the sight of the gentleman. Seeing Lord Finlington made him feel significantly less alone and vulnerable. But he felt sick at the thought that the viscount would be ashamed of him for going to see Jack in the first place.

"And that handsome man from the Fox & Thistle," Lord Finlington continued. "My goodness me, what a reunion. To what do I owe the pleasure, gentlemen?"

"I'm here to collect what is owed to me," Jack said. "Pip

said he wanted to pay off his debt. Told me to name my price."

Pip winced.

"Ah," Lord Finlington said blithely. "Well, I daresay that explains a great deal. I take it that my being here rather complicates things for you, doesn't it? So, it's to be Pip's life or his payment?"

"That's the size of it. And I don't want money from you, not this time. I want that quizzing glass."

"Oh, is that all?" the viscount said, without even a moment's hesitation. Pip had a sudden certainty that the gentleman would have responded that way regardless of the price Jack had named. "Gladly." Then he flipped open the box by his side and pulled out the gold glass. He held it out, chain draping between his fingers.

"I don't think so," Jack snarled. "And then you'll pull him to safety and keep them both. Do I look foolish to you? You'll toss it on the ground so I can pick it up. Gently, now. If it breaks, so does he."

Lord Finlington arched an eyebrow at the request but hopped off the desk and slid the quizzing glass across the floor.

"Pick it up," Jack said in Pip's ear, shoving him to his knees again.

As Pip leaned over to pick up the quizzing glass, he realized several things at once. The first thing was that he knew Jack would not keep his word upon receiving the quizzing glass. He would either kill Pip in front of the viscount as revenge for imagined wrongs or he would take Pip back with him.

The next two things he realized were that he did not want to go back and, furthermore, he very much did not want to die.

Then, as he slowly moved forward, careful not to lean into the knife blade, he also realized a willow branch was jutting out from under the nearest wingback chair and mere inches away from the quizzing glass. Pip was fairly sure it hadn't been there when the quizzing glass was slid across the floor.

It was then that Pip realized the final thing: Lord Finlington still trusted him, even after all of his shameful mistakes.

It was all of these realizations that gave Pip the courage to scoop up the willow branch and the quizzing glass in the same movement, spin on his knees away from the blade at his throat, braving the painful grip on his hair, and shove the wind spell up and at Jack Reid.

Pip knew as soon as he had cast it that he had overshot. He could feel the power, fueled by his anger and his fear, even before it coursed through the willow branch. This was confirmed when Jack, surprised by the gust that rammed into him from nowhere, dropped the knife and lost his grip on Pip's hair. Jack hit the ceiling with a loud whack, which startled Pip so much that he let go of the spell. This caused Jack to then fall to the floor with a great thump. He didn't move.

Pip leaned forward to check if Jack was alive but was forestalled by a gentle hand on his shoulder. "No, no, darling. Allow me."

Lord Finlington slid one elegant shoe under Jack's shoulder and, with surprising strength, kicked Jack over onto his back. He leaned over and touched two fingers to Jack's neck. "Mm," he said, straightening. "Still alive. Remarkable, really, considering he hit his head twice. Shame. Although I am glad you will be spared having his death on your conscience."

He reached into his pocket and pulled out a small tube, which he uncorked and overturned onto Jack's head. A fine powder floated down. "There," the viscount said. "That should take care of him until we can find out what to do."

"We have to help Lino," Pip said, stumbling to his feet and then swaying a bit in his hurry.

Lord Finlington put a solicitous hand under Pip's arm to keep him steady. "They're all gone, darling. I have a spell on my windows to fill all intruders with terror if they don't come inside right away. You've seen it in action before, I think. The last time you came to my house, the man who helped you break in was not there when you left."

Pip thought back to the night of the first break-in and how Tom was missing when he and Nell left the townhouse.

"They all fled in different directions while you were still unlocking the door. I expect the young man you were worried about—Lino, was it?—was able to escape when he was no longer being held at knifepoint."

"He tried to save me, my lord. I have to—"

"I will find him as soon as I'm assured of your wellbeing. All right?"

Pip nodded.

"Come along, my sweet. Let's get you bathed and fed. I daresay you've had quite the harrowing evening, poor thing."

Pip was too exhausted to argue. He was given a deliciously warm bath that did much to ease his aching feet and the soreness in his limbs from walking through the cold city.

After his bath, Lord Finlington's valet applied tinctures to Pip's feet and neck. Pip recognized the bottles as the same kind that held the lavender liquid he took for sleep. He guessed that the viscount had sent them up with instructions on where to apply them. He was horribly embarrassed that the viscount had noticed the bruises Jack's lips had left on Pip's neck, but he was grateful for the consideration all the same.

He was given dinner in bed and felt guilty by how pampered he felt by all of it. He didn't deserve such kindness, but he was too tired, too sore, and too ashamed to bring himself to talk to the viscount about the evening's events. A vial of purple liquid was sent up to his room before he went to sleep. He wondered a little at the viscount's ability to anticipate his needs in such a way, but he drifted off to sleep before he had come up with a viable reason.

The next morning, he woke to find the dukex sitting in his room with a book in their lap. "How are you feeling, poppet?"

Pip swallowed the lump in his throat. "I'm so sorry," he whispered.

"Hush now," they said. "It's all right. Bertram wanted to speak to you when you were awake. Shall I let him in?"

Pip very much did not want to face the viscount but couldn't very well refuse, so he nodded.

When Lord Finlington entered the room, the first thing he said was, "I wish to tell you, m'dear, that I've handed over that wretched man to the constabulary. You won't have to worry about him anymore. I also want to inform you that your friend, Lino, made it safely away. He came back, actually, to make sure you were all right. And," he went on, before Pip could comment on any of this, "your things have all been packed for home."

"Oh, but, sir," Pip said, pushing himself up to sit. "Gerry's supplies—I couldn't possibly—"

The viscount held up a hand. "Not to worry, darling. I'm going out shopping for everything this morning."

Pip slumped against the pillows, weighed down by his failures.

"Don't misunderstand me, dearest. I don't mean to suggest that you are unable to purchase them yourself. After all, you did a marvelous job of it yesterday. But you really are quite wrung out. I don't wish you to exert yourself. If I may be so bold as to suggest that you take another dosage of the sleeping draught, I think it would be most helpful to you."

"Yes, my lord."

"Don't hesitate to ring for the servants if you need anything at all. All right? Julian will be here to look after you. I'll be back before lunch and we'll head home immediately."

Pip nodded, even though the gentleman was already walking out of the room. He took the recommended dosage, deciding that the very least he owed the viscount was to listen to the man's advice. As such, he woke up in the carriage, his head on someone's shoulder, too tired to raise his head and find out who the shoulder belonged to.

Lord Finlington explained to him, in kind tones, that he had been too drowsy to be awakened for the trip downstairs. "I do not mean to abscond with you, of course," he added hastily. "But it really seemed criminal to wake you after all you've been through."

Pip wanted to tell the viscount that he deserved every bit of what he'd been through, but he was already falling back asleep, lulled by both the vial's magic and the rocking of the carriage. Later, he was vaguely aware of being lifted out of the carriage, into a house and up the stairs, but he was hardly able to register any of it. Gentle hands gave him another dosage of the sleeping draught and he slept until the sun was high above the trees in Tutting-on-Cress.

CHAPTER 20

PIP WOKE AGAIN to see the dukex sitting beside his bed.

"You came back," he said drowsily.

The dukex looked up from their book and smiled at him. "Of course I did, child. Didn't I tell you I'd look after you like you were my own?"

"You shouldn't have had to."

"There's no place I'd rather be right now, poppet."

Pip rubbed his face and looked around the room. "We're in Charles's house?"

"Yes."

"Oh," he said, with a sinking feeling. "But their honeymoon."

The dukex raised an eyebrow. "Do you really think either of them would have forgiven us if we'd taken you anywhere else?"

Pip allowed himself a weak chuckle at that. "I suppose not. Is Gerry here too?"

"Yes. She came back as soon as Bertram delivered the supplies to her. Would you like me to send for some food?"

Pip shook his head. "I'd better go downstairs and talk to Gerry before she leaves for work."

But by the time Pip made it downstairs, Gerry had already

left for the shop. He wasn't surprised, although the sharp pang of shame blossomed again in his chest. He could barely bring himself to meet Charles and Gavin's eyes while they sat with him for his late breakfast. They did not ask him about his trip, for which he was grateful. However, there was a part of him that wanted to confess. He had so much to atone for now, even more than he had before moving to the country. He felt sure unburdening his heart was the least he owed his friends, but he could not bring himself to say the words. He could not bear to speak of his foolishness in going to Jack, or speak of the way Jack had touched him, or how he'd prized Lord Finlington's treasures over his own worthless self. He was dreading the next encounter with Gerry after failing at the task he had offered to do. He was dizzy in his misery.

After a very long silence, he finally had the courage to say, "I'm very sorry your honeymoon was cut short."

Gavin shook his head before Pip had even finished the sentence. "Your safety is far more important, Pip."

"But you barely had any opportunity for privacy."

"We have the rest of our lives together," Charles said. "Besides, we have our own room. I do not require an entire house to make love to my husband."

Gavin turned bright red. "*Charles.*"

Pip gave a small smile at this. "I suppose if you really do need the entire house, after the dukex leaves, you will have most days while Gerry and I are at the shop."

"Exactly!" Charles said. "Plenty of opportunities for everything I intend to do, not to mention whatever Gavin might have in mind." He smiled as Gavin choked a little on his tea. "I can safely promise that I will take every advantage of that if it will make you feel better."

Pip nodded. It wasn't enough, but it would have to suffice.

After breakfast, he escaped to the garden, but the quiet of nature did not calm his spirits as it usually did. He finally sank onto a stone bench, wishing he was back in bed, and feeling guilty for being so exhausted.

The dukex found him some time later. "Bertram is here," they said. "But you needn't go inside until you're ready. He wished to see for himself that you were all right."

Pip nodded but didn't move from his seat. "Thank you," he added belatedly.

The dukex sat down beside him. "Do you wish to talk about it?"

"I'm not sure how," he admitted. "I've been so…so foolish." And before he could stop himself, he started crying.

The dukex gathered him up in a tight hug. "Of course you haven't," they said. "Tell me what happened."

After his tears subsided, he told them, haltingly, about his dreadful experience in London, from the shopping trip, to the tavern, to Jack holding him, to his decision to give Jack the quizzing glass, and ending with the viscount's presence at the townhouse and how Jack ended up unconscious. Throughout the tale, the dukex rubbed his back soothingly. Pip was relieved that they never pulled away from him in disgust.

When he was done, they said, "What a dreadful ordeal, my dear. I'm so sorry you had to go through all that. But you mustn't blame yourself."

Pip sniffed, his head on their shoulder. "I should never have gone to that tavern. I should have taken that spell his lordship gave me and gotten away. It was idiotic of me. I don't know how I shall ever make up for it."

"You are most certainly not idiotic. After all, didn't you say Bertram placed that bit of willow under the chair for you? He wouldn't have done that if he didn't trust you to do what was needed."

Pip considered this. "I've been thinking about that, too," he said at last. "It was very kind of him to give me the chance to take care of matters."

"And you did. You did the right thing in the end. That's

what matters. And your decision to go to the tavern was well-intentioned, if nothing else. Now you can finally put that chapter of your life to rest."

"I thought you'd be ashamed of me," Pip admitted.

The dukex tutted. "Nonsense, child. You've done nothing to be ashamed of."

If it had been anyone else, Pip might have argued. But since it was the dukex, he didn't quite dare contradict them. Finally, he pulled away from their embrace. "Thank you for listening," he said. "I suppose I should go inside. I'm probably keeping you from your lunch."

"Lunch will do you some good too, child," they said. "And Bertram will want to see you, if you're up to more conversation."

"I don't think I could bear to face him," Pip said. "I can't imagine what he must think of me."

"Oh, poppet," they said on a sigh. "I can assure you he isn't in the least bit upset or disappointed in you, only worried."

"I was sent to London to do one simple thing," Pip said. "I couldn't even do that. His lordship had to—" He broke off.

"What is it, child?"

He frowned, thinking furiously about past conversations.

"Are you all right?"

He stood. "Excuse me, Your Grace. I think I need to talk to his lordship."

"I believe he's waiting in the library."

He went straight to the library, where he found Lord Finlington chatting with Charles. When Pip entered the room, they both stood.

"How are you feeling, darling?" the viscount asked at the same time Charles said, "Are you ready for some lunch, my dear?"

Pip shook his head. "I'm so sorry," he said. "My lord, do

you think I could talk to you for a moment?" He hesitated. "Alone?"

"To be sure, m'dear," Lord Finlington said.

Charles did not ask any questions. He got up and walked out of the room, shutting the door behind him.

Pip couldn't bring himself to meet the viscount's gaze. He stared at the floor and took a deep breath. "I wanted to ask you about something you said before we left London."

"Of course, my sweet. Here, do sit down." He bustled over and gently directed Pip toward the settee.

Pip sat and folded his hands in his lap, clenching them tightly. He was dreading the answer to the question he intended to ask. "When you went to go buy the supplies for Gerry...you mentioned that I had done a fine job of it myself." He dared a glance up at the gentleman. "But Jack took all the packages away from me. So how did you know about that?"

The viscount looked, to Pip's surprise and confusion, a little guilty. "Ah. Yes. You see, well, I do hope you won't be too upset, darling. But I was a trifle worried about you wandering around on your own. I've had a notion that you might wish to pay off your debt with that man, considering how much money you had with you. And I was very worried that such an encounter would not go well. I'd been checking in on you from time-to-time with that scrying spell. When you left Smelting's, I saw those men surround you. After that, I watched the whole thing to make sure you would get out all right. I left my club as soon as I saw who you'd been brought to. I was actually halfway there when they pulled the knife on young Lino. But really you took care of everything just fine without me. You even handled yourself well with that beastly man holding you."

"You watched...all of that?" Pip felt his face flush.

"Yes, dear. I do hope you're not angry with me—"

Pip burst into tears, mortified at the prospect that the

viscount had witnessed his colossal mistakes and his shameful conversation with Jack. And he was thoroughly annoyed that now simply everyone he knew at Tutting-on-Cress had seen him cry. He supposed it was inevitable.

"Oh, you poor sweet thing, oh my," Lord Finlington said, opening his arms to Pip in silent invitation.

Pip accepted the comfort, folding into the viscount's arms, resting his head on his shoulder, and wrapping his arms around the gentleman's back. The viscount held him in a way that was gentle and firm, reassuring and comforting, all at once.

"How can you even look at me?" Pip said into the viscount's shoulder. "You saw how he touched me. You saw how foolish I was."

"Foolish? Darling, no! How can you say so? Good heavens. You had no choice when they surrounded you. Anyone could have seen that."

Pip's tears subsided enough for him to pull away. "I could have used the protection spell and I didn't."

"Well," the viscount said with a small smile. "It would have been a trifle difficult to get to. You did stash it deep into that pocket."

"They would have picked it otherwise."

Lord Finlington huffed. "Well, that really is my fault, dearest. I ought to have explained that it was warded against that sort of thing."

Pip's eyes widened. "But Jack took it out, right out of my pocket."

"Yes, but he had to tug it to get it out, didn't he? No one would have been able to sneak it out of your possession. I really should have mentioned it. Can you ever forgive me, darling?"

"Forgive? My lord, can you ever forgive *me*? I brought him back. I brought him back fully intending to give him that quizzing glass. I completely betrayed your trust, even after all you've done for me."

"Well, you didn't exactly have many options, did you, my sweet? Quite frankly, you made the wisest choice you could. Bringing him back to my house was the smartest possible solution, for there are all sorts of protection spells in place. And, of course, I hope you know that your life is worth far more to me than that silly quizzing glass." He pulled a handkerchief out of his breast pocket and tenderly wiped Pip's face. "The question is, dearest, have I completely betrayed your trust? I know when you helped me with the scrying spell, you said you didn't mind, but I'm sure you had no idea I would use it in such—"

Pip laid a hand on the gentleman's wrist, halting the attempts to dry his face. "You have saved my life so many times and in so many ways. There is no one I would rather have keeping an eye on me than you, Bertie."

The viscount's smile was radiant. "My darling man," he said. "Do you know that I absolutely adore you?"

Pip had a feeling the moment would have been well sealed with a kiss, but he was a trifle terrified by the prospect. He was relieved when Bertie didn't lean forward to initiate one.

Instead, Pip said, "There's something I've been wondering."

"Yes, dearest?"

"What does that quizzing glass do?"

To his surprise, Bertie threw back his head and laughed. "You know, darling, I have absolutely no idea."

Pip gaped. Bertie gave a shrug. "Haven't the foggiest notion. I know it to be a magical tool of some kind, possibly very powerful and undoubtedly invaluable, but I have yet to discern what sort. I brought it back home with me."

"Home? You mean here? You're staying?"

Bertie smiled. "My family is here, darling. There isn't anywhere else I'd call home."

Pip sighed in relief. "I'm glad. I thought you might go back to London."

"Well, I had every intention to. But really, I quite like it here. I'm certainly not lacking in entertainment with you darlings living so close. And I have plenty of experiments to do at home. I think the quizzing glass will make a nice project someday. Won't it be fun figuring out what it does?"

"May I help?" Pip said tentatively.

"I was hoping you'd ask."

Pip ducked his head. "Not soon, I think. I feel as though I ought to earn that right. I have so much to atone for."

Bertie gently slid Pip's hand into his and said, "Do you know, petal, that you have had me wrapped around your little finger," he tapped the tip of Pip's pinky, "ever since you flashed that perfect smile at me the night we met? So don't fret about any sort of atonement. I count myself lucky just to have your friendship."

Pip reached up with his free hand and traced Bertie's mouth with his thumb. The viscount's lips were soft and smiling under the touch. It was not a kiss, but it was enough for Pip to know that Bertie would never ask more of him than he was ready to give. Once more, he folded himself into the man's arms and stayed there, safe, for a long time.

Afterward, they joined Charles, Gavin, Gerry, and the dukex for lunch. When Gerry greeted Pip with a tight hug, he felt the last of his anxieties about the trip start to melt away. Everyone very pointedly did not comment on the length of time Pip and Bertie had been talking alone in the study.

∼

HE FOUND HIMSELF VISITING BERTIE'S HOUSE MORE AND MORE IN the following months. The dukex left as soon as they were assured Pip was well. As the dukex had predicted, Charles was a highly indulgent sort of chaperone, who not only didn't object to Pip going to visit Bertie unescorted, but frequently encouraged such visits. Pip found he was becoming gradually less shy around the elegant viscount.

Once again, Pip discovered a shift in one of his friendships. Bertie was still fastidious about not touching Pip more than was absolutely necessary, but Pip started to show the viscount what made him feel comfortable. It was nothing like the sort of affection Jack had once shown him; there were no kisses, or strokes, or even many embraces. It became a new sort of education, teaching himself what he wanted and needed. Although Pip was fairly sure he was falling in love with Bertie, he was not yet ready for that to be a certainty.

Without discussing it, he knew Bertie understood. He knew it in the way Bertie never initiated more than a touch to his arm without encouragement. So Pip took it upon himself to reach for the viscount's hand while Bertie showed him around the garden, or lean his head on the viscount's shoulder anytime they sat alone in a room together. He looked forward to the day when Bertie might brush a hand through Pip's hair without dragging up a rush of painful memories, but there was no hurry to get there.

And Pip realized one quiet evening, as he sat tucked against Bertie in his sitting room, with his friend's arm draped over his shoulder, that he still had plenty to enjoy until then.

The End

NOTE FROM THE AUTHOR

DEAR READER,

I started this story while I was still in the middle of another. Pip was a character I added to *One Good Turn* with the intention of making him an incidental character who showed up for two or three scenes. But then I wrote a scene where Jack petted Pip and immediately recognized the relationship as abusive. Instead of changing the relationship, I thought "oh no. I need to save him!" and spent a lot of time trying to finish Nell's story but mentally writing Pip's. I wound up pausing book 2 until book 3 was fully drafted.

For me, this story is about the power of fresh starts, found family, and how depression can warp the way our minds work. Some of Pip's thought spirals are replicas of my own, and it was important for Pip to have space to heal and a support network to help him as he did.

I hope you enjoyed reading his journey as much as I enjoyed writing it.

Affectionately,
Sarah Wallace

ACKNOWLEDGMENTS

As ever, this book wouldn't exist without my own amazing support network. To Ashley, who acted as my sounding board way back when this was one half of another book, this story wouldn't exist without your feedback (and thank you for pointing out when I paralleled *Jurassic Park*—that was a surprising twist!). To Alexis, thank you for telling me what worked and for reading every iteration this book has taken. To Kayla, thank you for pushing me to give Pip his own book. To my editor, Mackenzie, thank you for encouraging me to write more scenes with Pip and Bertie together. I hadn't realized how much they were needed until they were written. To my beta readers, Katie, Allison, Karen, and Kay, thank you so much for all of your feedback. You helped me shape this book into what it is today! And to my amazing readers, thank you for sticking with me—and an extra thanks to those who have been looking forward to Pip's book. I hope it lived up to your expectations!

Editor: Mackenzie Walton
Proofreader: Ashley Scout
Historical Consultant: Alexis Howard
Front and back cover photo by Annie Spratt via Unsplash
Author photos by Toni Tillman

ABOUT THE AUTHOR

 Sarah Wallace lives in Florida with her cat, more books than she has time to read, a large collection of classic movies, and an apartment full of plants that are surviving against all odds. She only reads books that end happily.

ALSO BY SARAH WALLACE

Letters to Half Moon Street

One Good Turn

The Glamour Spell of Rose Talbot - free to all newsletter subscribers!

Next in Meddle & Mend

Dear

Bartleby

Coming in Autumn 2023

PREVIEW FOR LETTERS TO HALF MOON STREET

FROM GERALDINE HARTFORD
Shulfield Hall, Tutting-on-Cress
TO GAVIN HARTFORD
8 Half Moon Street, London

28 August 1815

DEAR GAVIN,

Mama has written to me about her scheme to send you to London. I thought having a letter waiting for you when you arrive might be a pleasant surprise. You will likely be a grump about the whole thing for you do not enjoy having your life upset, but surely you will not want to be at home when John and Veronica take over the house. You and John have never gotten along in the best of circumstances. Living together while his wife goes through her confinement will only exacerbate things. Goodness knows what sort of chaos will ensue when her baby is actually born. Mama is quite right to send you away. You know I do not say that lightly.

Before you ask, no, I will not come and help you settle in London. I am having a capital time with our cousins and have no interest in leaving.

I believe living alone in town will do you some good. You want a little independence, my dear brother. Please do not spend all of your time in the library.

And do try to enjoy yourself.

Affectionately,

Gerry

FROM GAVIN HARTFORD
   8 Half Moon Street, London
TO GERALDINE HARTFORD
   Shulfield Hall, Tutting-on-Cress

1 September 1815

GERRY,

London is already a right bore. If you were a kind sister, like you ought to be, you would not make me suffer alone. Terribly unsporting of you.

Mother was in a fine state before I left. She had the servants going through all the usual household spells, making sure every part of the house was spotless. I don't see why she bothers. Veronica is happiest when she feels superior, so a less than perfect house will make her more eager than ever to be mistress of it someday.

When Mother first suggested this scheme, I thought she was sending me to London only to get me out of the house temporarily. But it seems she intends for me to stay until after the baby is born. She even said I might as well stay for six months or more. She has insisted I will be in the way. It is absurd for her to be in such a state. Veronica is unlikely to actually take Mother's advice on anything, and will only frustrate everybody.

Oh, and Father sat me down and went over all of the business he wants me to take care of while I am in London. I suppose I should be grateful he did not foist these responsibilities upon me sooner. And I daresay I'm glad I'm not the firstborn. Having that much responsibility would be even worse, even with the benefit of inheritance. At any rate, Father said the real reason I am staying here is to see to it that the townhouse is prepared for the Season, and he gave me a list of things he wants taken care of. He also said if I do well enough at all of this, I might be able to continue with it as an actual career—acting as steward on John's behalf. I shudder to imagine it. I really must find an occupation for myself, and soon. I did notice Father did not alter the timeline Mother put forth. So I suspect this list of responsibilities is merely to keep me busy. What a great bother it all is.

Our townhouse in London was outrageously warm when I arrived. I'm glad I wasn't sent here at the height of the summer. As it was, I had to dash around the house to help the servants open the windows. Then I had to set up at least a dozen cooling spells. Cook already needs more mint for the purpose. I still have that tendency to overload my spells with too much magical power, so the cooling spells ought to have made the place frigid. And yet, it is still too warm. It would be far better if you were here to help me.

I confess I am thoroughly intimidated by the city. Father gave me directions to the club we're members of. I had initially planned to walk there. I'm accustomed to walking or riding everywhere back at home, but I am far too nervous about getting lost. I took a hackney the first time I went to Nesbit's Club, and I was immediately confused by all the turns and the traffic. I am sure you will scold me, but I cannot countenance going anywhere other than the club at this juncture.

Did you go to Nesbit's when you were in town? I own I did not know what to expect. I liked the quiet atmosphere, but I was alarmed by the number of people inside. I went straight to the dining room and found a little table in the corner. I sat next to a lovely stained glass window, which was pleasant, and no one approached me, which was a relief. It was unsettling, though, to sit in a dining room amongst strangers and to be completely alone.

Now I am alone in London and it may be months before I can leave. Until the Season begins in earnest, there is precious little to do. Not that I would relish being here when the Season is at its peak, for you know I do not enjoy suffering through so much society. Even with Father's list of responsibilities, I am not exactly busy. I daresay I'm grateful for that, but I feel sure I shall forget something. Practically all I have to occupy my time is to dine at Nesbit's Club, which is hardly diverting. At home, I could hide in books all day, but the library in our London house is nothing to the library at home. It would serve our parents right if I gambled away my funds out of sheer boredom.

Give my regards to our cousins.

Affectionately,
Gavin

FROM GERALDINE HARTFORD
Shulfield Hall, Tutting-on-Cress
TO GAVIN HARTFORD
8 Half Moon Street, London

4 September 1815

DEAR GAVIN,

You know Mama. Once she has a scheme in her head she must have her way.

Do you remember when our cousin said Tutting-on-Cress was simply filled with eligible bachelors? Now that I am here, I am convinced Rose was fibbing. There are precious few single men around. Besides, I'm fairly sure Rose fancies another woman in the village. So I have no idea why she was even considering gentlemen suitors. From what Aunt Lily has said, there was some sort of to-do in the spring—something about a dashing bachelor. Rose has been tight-lipped on the details, but I suppose it's possible for her to be of the feminine persuasion and still have her head turned by a particularly handsome man. If I learn more, I shall tell you.

In any case, attempting to win a husband is an exhausting experience. So I'm not opposed to simply enjoying my time here, rather than continuing the search. I have not admitted any of this to Mama yet. I think she will be disappointed about the lack of prospective suitors, but I doubt she will mind me staying here indefinitely. She trusts me to behave well around John even less than she trusts you. You will simply grumble and lock yourself up in the library. But suffering under John's company, I might actually put a curse on him, brother or no.

You cannot convince me there is nothing for you to do. Is there no one you can talk to at our club? You do know Nesbit's caters to the intellectual set, don't you? I'm sure you could find someone there who shares an interest in poetry or magic or something. Of course, you would have to actually talk to them to discover this. I certainly hope you do not intend to spend your entire time in London without talking to anybody.

I agree with you on the subject of the library in the townhouse. Try Hatchard's Bookshop. They kept me quite afloat while I was in London.

I don't believe you would be such a pinhead as to gamble away your money. But I think it might do you some good to be reckless, so I will not talk you out of it. I warn you, however, that I shall not lend you my money. The shops in Tutting-on-Cress are excellent, despite it being a small town, and there are plenty of things I wish to buy.

Affectionately,

Gerry

FROM GAVIN HARTFORD
   8 Half Moon Street, London
TO GERALDINE HARTFORD
   Shulfield Hall, Tutting-on-Cress

7 September 1815

GERRY,

You may not believe it, but I have already completed Father's list. Well, some of the items must be repeated throughout my stay, but I have managed to take care of everything else. I suppose Father may be right about this being a suitable career for me. I mean to say, I did not find anything he had me do at all difficult. I might even consider it as a viable option, but I truly cannot countenance having to answer to John for the rest of my life. I have a suspicion Father knows this and is looking to oust me from my current state of indecision.

I am sure I would not mind finding a career for myself, but I haven't the faintest idea of what I should do. I am not clever enough for law, nor to be a professor. I'm sure I haven't the stomach to be a doctor, nor the proper gravity to be a vicar. And I know what you shall say: I have more than enough gravity. You take my meaning. I have not the soul of a vicar. Besides, vicars have to talk a great deal to people quite regularly and I'm sure I should hate that. Come to think of it, law poses the same problem. So does the medical profession. And teaching. Blast it. I wish I could be like you and Seb and simply look for a spouse. But the very notion of such a task fills me with utter dread. I want to retch just thinking about it.

My evenings at the club have been very strange lately. The manager keeps asking me if I would like to be introduced to people. Did she ever do that to you? I told her I knew no one in London, and then she said apparently some people would like to know me. This was a terrifying prospect, so I begged her to discourage them as politely as she could. She gave me an odd look but did as I asked. I have taken to practically inhaling my food in order to prevent this from happening again. I would take my meals at home but it is far too hot for such a thing.

If you were here, we could make a merry party of it at the club together. I'm sure you will tell me you have acquaintances in town and you would be perfectly happy to meet new people. Even if I were forced to suffer through some amount of society, it would be far less horrifying if I had someone to do it all with me.

Is there no chance I can persuade you to come stay in London?

Affectionately,

Gavin

READ THE REST OF LETTERS TO HALF MOON STREET, *AVAILABLE AT all retailers.*

PREVIEW FOR ONE GOOD TURN

THE DAY that ultimately changed Nell Birks's life started as a rather ordinary one.

She had gone to work at Smelting's Spell Shop, one of her various odd-jobs. Of all of these odd-jobs, Nell liked working at Smelting's best of all. Though the work was less creative and more mundane than many of the other jobs she did, and Smelting—mean old crank that he was—paid her poorly, it was a good sight better than being a thief and forever looking over her shoulder.

On a chilly day between winter and spring, Nell was sweeping the shop briskly while Mr. Smelting worked in the back room. Her task was disrupted by a toff who strode into the store and looked about as if he were a little lost. He was tall with broad, muscled shoulders. He had large, dark, angular eyes, a wide nose, strong jaw, and wide mouth. His skin was tan in color, but Nell was sure it was not the result of too many hours in the sun; he was far too finely dressed to be the type who worked outdoors, and too finely dressed to be mucking about in her corner of London, for that matter. She recognized the elegant stitching of his coat, the curl of his hat brim, and the crispness of his cravat for what they were: quality. She groaned inwardly. She'd seen gents of his ilk before, although admittedly they weren't usually shopping for spells. Usually, they were looking for some cheap pleasure or to hawk some family heirloom to pay off creditors.

So she was surprised when the gentleman smiled at her and said, "Good morning, friend. I'm looking to buy some ingredients, but unfortunately, I have little understanding of these things." This was said with a self-deprecating smile. "I would be very grateful if you could assist."

Nell was taken aback by how readily the gentleman accepted her as a source of knowledge. She couldn't decide if his mistake made him seem foolish or kind.

She shook her head. "I'd better fetch Smelting for you." His grin broadened. "Much obliged."

As promised, she fetched Smelting, a short and scrawny older man with leathery skin. As soon as the spellmaster was out of the backroom, Nell did what she normally did and pocketed a few discarded items. She enjoyed being surrounded by magic work. She had never admitted this fascination with anyone else; they would have scoffed at her for wanting something so above her own station.

Nell had crafted her own education from observing Smelting's work and the street magicians who did the flashy sort of spells that people paid money to see. She had mastered a few spells: one that temporarily made things weightless, a persuasion spell, and her favorite—a look-away spell. She was most proud of the last one, because she had worked it out on her own. She had seen a street magician performing a spell to turn things invisible and tried to mimic it. Though she had never successfully turned anything invisible, in attempting to teach herself the invisibility spell, she had discovered that twisting her wrist in a certain way could sometimes cast a spell that made people not *quite* notice her.

She tucked a small sprig of rosemary in her left pocket (good for both the persuasion spell and the look-away spell).

When she found a slightly crumpled feather in the corner

of the room, still fluffy enough to be useful for the spell that made things weightless, she stowed it safely in her shirt pocket. Smelting always let things go to waste.

She strode through the backroom swiftly, keeping an ear to the conversation in the shop. The gentleman shopper didn't seem to know very much about magic.

"And what spell is this item used for?" he asked Smelting. "Is it dangerous? Does it need to be treated? This looks interesting. What is it? Is it useful? Do you have any ingredients that might be harder for a spellcaster to acquire? This is quite a pretty flower. Is it—oh, what a shame."

She wondered why he had bothered to come all this way if he was so inexperienced.

She came out of the backroom and returned to her sweeping, trying not to be obvious in her eavesdropping. She had a bad feeling about the gentleman coming into the shop. Not only did people of his station rarely meander to the neighborhood, they rarely still made it out with their purses. Sometimes they never made it out at all. The ones who made a practice of coming to the brothels knew to at least cover themselves with shabby cloaks to appear slightly less conspicuous. But this bloke carried his wealth easily on his shoulders. She was frankly surprised he had survived to the shop in the first place.

Nell ducked outside to see if the customer had attracted any hopeful stragglers. Sure enough, her best friend Philip Standish was hovering near the door with Davey Smith and the Connor twins. Philip, who everyone called Pip, had been her closest friend since they were little, having met while they were learning pickpocketing from Jack Reid. Jack found her as an orphan begging on the street and began teaching her the trade. But as she grew older, she wanted to do more honest work.

As children, she had always been Pip's protector. He was the closest thing to family Nell had. When she told Jack she wanted to find work honestly, she had expected Pip to follow. But he didn't. Now Pip worked in one of Jack's many groups of thieves who took by force. She barely saw him anymore, so she was pleased enough by the sight of her friend to step out of the shop.

"Morning, Nelly," Pip said, grinning up at her.

"Morning, Pip. What are you lot doing around here?"

"Didn't you see that toff inside?" Jimmy said.

She shrugged. "So?"

"You must be rustier than I thought," Davey said, leaning against the building. "If you can't spot a mark like that a mile away."

"I don't know about that one," she said slowly. "Seemed a little too fine, if you ask me."

Davey scoffed. "Too fine, indeed. Deep purses like that don't come wandering through our streets just any old time. Or haven't you noticed?"

"Of course I noticed," she retorted. "I may be rusty, but I'm not an idiot. What I'm saying is that one in there is too fine to be the type to carry his purse around with him. And he's far too fine to be a nobody."

Davey rolled his eyes. "I don't care if he's the Prince Regent, himself. Whatever he's got will put me in Jack's good graces for a month or more. I ain't about to pass that up."

"More fool you," she said.

"What do you mean, Nelly?" Pip said, crossing his arms. "What's got you keyed up?"

"Sweet on him, isn't she?" Jimmy said, elbowing Pip with a wink. Pip ducked his head.

Nell rolled her eyes. "Not likely. All I'm saying—"

It was a shame, really, that the gentleman came out when he did. Nell was pretty sure she had the boys close to her way of thinking. If he had stayed inside a few minutes more, she might have convinced them that he wasn't worth their time

and she could have discreetly seen him to the respectable

side of town. As it was, he came out before she'd finished having her say. He was holding several packages in one arm. Nell realized he had bought raw supplies, rather than packaged spells, which surprised her a little.

"Oh," the gentleman said brightly, as if he didn't have a care in the world. "Good day, friends. Pardon me, won't you?"

He made as if to scoot past their group, but Davey was blocking his way in an instant.

"Not so fast, gov'nor," he said smoothly.

Jimmy reached behind Nell and pulled the shop door shut.

"You look as if you've got quite a ways to travel," Davey continued. "I'm thinking your purse will be weighing you down a bit. Don't you think, lads?"

The Connor twins chuckled appreciatively.

Nell ought to have given the stranger up for lost and gone back inside, but she didn't. She couldn't explain why she was so determined to see him safe. Perhaps it had been the way he had easily accepted her as someone worthy of his time and respect. Or perhaps it was the cheerful way he greeted everyone, as if everyone he met was a friend.

Before she could think better of it, she stepped between Davey and the gentleman.

"What's this?" Davey said.

"Like I was telling you before," she said. "I think you should leave off this one."

Davey sneered. "Want him for yourself, do you?"

"You know I don't do that anymore."

"Told you she was sweet on him," Jimmy said.

Nell surreptitiously slipped her hand into her left pocket and palmed the sprig of rosemary. She eased her hand back out and did a little swishing motion by her side. "Come on now, Davey. You know me better than that. I don't think this one's a good idea."

She could tell the persuasion spell started to activate when Davey took a step back. "And why not?" he asked, belligerent.

She leaned forward as if imparting a big secret. "Don't ask why, but something about this one's manner tells me: judge's son. If you take this one, I'll bet you anything you'll be swinging within a fortnight."

"If they can catch me," Davey said, but he seemed a little less certain now.

"You think he came all this way without telling his pa where he went?" she persisted, grateful that the man in question hadn't been foolish enough to interrupt. She didn't dare look back at him to see how he was reacting. "Let this one off, Davey. He's not worth the risk."

The spell took hold of Pip first. He tugged on Davey's arm. "She's right. Let's go."

Davey's eyes darted between Nell and the gentleman. Finally, he relented. The group stalked off.

Nell pocketed the rosemary and grabbed the gentleman's wrist. "Come on, sir," she whispered. "Before they get wise."

With an expression that seemed equal parts amused and bemused, the gentleman complied.

When she reached the wider streets that marked the safer part of London, she rounded on the gentleman. "You know you almost had your throat slit," she said.

The statement did not have the effect she intended. The gentleman did not look at all horrified, mainly curious. "Indeed?" he said. "I daresay I'm in your debt then, aren't I, my dear?"

She frowned. "Not hardly. Just take care you don't go wandering around that part of town again. I can't guarantee I'll be there next time. Or that the spell will work again."

"Ah, so you *were* working magic." He seemed pleased to have noticed. "What sort of spell was that? I can't say I've ever seen it before."

She huffed. "It's a persuasion spell. Now, if you'll excuse me, I'd better get back to my work."

"Oh, just a moment," he said, with a hand on her shoulder.

Nell sighed and turned around.

"Why did you stop them? Not that I'm not grateful, mind you. Simply curious. I'm not sure many would have bothered."

She wasn't entirely sure of the answer to the question, which made her uncomfortable. She shrugged. "Right thing to do, I suppose."

His mouth quirked. "How noble. Well, my dear. One good turn certainly deserves another. If you ever require my assistance, please do not hesitate to call. The name is Charles Kentworthy and I live at 16 Berkeley Square." He bowed to her as if she were a fine lady and walked away.

Nell stared at him, despite her need to head back to the shop. He really was a fool to give her his address. How could he know she wouldn't rob him? Overly trusting blighter. She supposed he wasn't entirely wrong to trust her, since she didn't plan to do anything with the information. He had given her his name, as if he considered her a friend. She was a little stunned by the whole interaction. She realized that she was reacting to him the way she expected him to react to her. Wasn't that just like the upper crust? To make her feel like he had done her a favor instead of the other way around.

"Well, where were you?" Mr. Smelting said when she finally walked back into the shop.

"That toff was lost. I helped him find his way back."

Smelting snorted. "I believe it. I don't think that one had been inside a spell shop in his life."

"What was he here for, then?"

"Oh, he bought a nice little bundle of ingredients. He asked all sorts of questions about what each one was good for."

She rolled her eyes. "I'll bet you charged him double."

Smelting frowned suddenly. "No," he said slowly. "He was good at haggling, actually. Knew how much each ought to cost."

She was as surprised as Smelting was by this revelation. But she proceeded to go about her work and tried to put the tall, friendly Kentworthy person out of her mind.

READ THE REST OF ONE GOOD TURN, AVAILABLE AT ALL RETAILERS.

SIGN UP FOR MY NEWSLETTER!

ARE you signed up for my newsletter? Join now at sarahwallacewriter.com to be in the know!

NEWSLETTER SUBSCRIBERS ARE THE FIRST TO SEE BOOK COVERS, receive the first chapter of new releases a month before release date, get sneak peeks at preorder campaign art, and a free novelette! I've also been known to send deleted scenes or scenes in alternate POV and I plan to do more of that!

READ ON FOR A PREVIEW OF THE FREE NOVELETTE *THE GLAMOUR Spell of Rose Talbot.*

PREVIEW FOR THE GLAMOUR
SPELL OF ROSE TALBOT

THE WHOLE AFFAIR began when Mr. Harry Bowden abandoned all apparent sense and fell in love with Miss Kitty Corley.

"It is the outside of enough," Rose Talbot groused to her friend, Julia Hearst. "Everyone knows that I have set my cap at Mr. Bowden. And everyone knows Miss Corley is the prettiest girl in Tutting-on-Cress. Why must she have everything?"

Julia Hearst took a bite of shortbread and did not reply. The two ladies were sitting in the drawing room, having tea. When Mr. Hearst had died two years ago, he had left his young wife in possession of a small cottage and a modest income. Julia was a sensible woman, sensible enough to manage on said modest income and sensible enough not to intervene when Rose was in a *mood*.

"I truly do not understand what everyone finds so special about Miss Corley," Rose continued. "Yes, she is utterly beautiful. Yes, she has the most perfectly golden hair with those perfectly tiny curls that frame her face just so. Yes, her eyes are very blue and her figure is very trim. And yes, she plays the pianoforte better than I do and has the voice of a veritable angel." Rose paused, having lost track of her argument. "Oh, bother," she said. "She's utterly perfect, of course. But, must she be all that *and* have secured Mr. Bowden's affections? It hardly seems fair."

Julia set her cup down and looked at her friend.

Rose had rather hoped that Julia would agree with her. Better yet, she'd hoped Julia would point out some of Miss Corley's faults. It would have made her feel far better about her circumstances if Julia would simply tell her that she was far superior to the new object of Mr. Bowden's affections. Unfortunately, Julia was simply looking patient and sympathetic, which was not nearly as satisfying.

"I know you are not fond of him," Rose said, finally giving up on expecting Julia to say what she wanted to hear. "But I do believe Mr. Bowden to be quite the most perfect gentleman of my acquaintance. He is clever, dark and mysterious, and he has a lovely smile. And I'm sure no one else has paid me the same attention that he has." She sighed. "What shall I do?"

"Perhaps," Julia said at last, "he is not worth your time, my dear, if he is so easily swayed. After all, to all appearances, he seemed about to propose to you only last month."

"Exactly!" Rose said, pointing with her biscuit for emphasis, a lapse in manners she would only dare in Julia's safe company. "I, for one, should like to know how she managed it."

"Then again," Julia continued quietly, "I seem to recall everyone being completely certain he would propose to Miss Worcester only last Season."

"Well, Lizzy Worcester's a bit of a ninnyhammer. I can't say I'm surprised by that turn of events. He probably just got her started on the right topic. You know how she gets."

"I rather like Lizzy," Julia said in a mild tone.

Rose opened her mouth to reply and then closed it. "Yes, I suppose she's all right," she said at last.

"I have always found it odd," Julia said, "that his interests invariably lay with the wealthiest ladies in the county."

"Oh, well, that is unfair," Rose said. "Is he not to inherit his father's fortune and title? I cannot believe him to be a fortune hunter. I am sure you are wrong."

"But three such different girls in the span of a year?" Julia persisted. "It is not normal."

"I seem to recall Lady Windham courting several young ladies in quick succession in much the same manner. Including your Miss Worcester," Rose said in a smug tone.

Julia sipped her tea. "Very true, my dear. But Caro Windham is hardly a good example. She has been married to Maria for over a year and is still one of the most brazen flirts I have ever encountered. Mr. Bowden may not be a fortune hunter, but he may well be another Lady Windham, in his way ."

Rose frowned at this observation. "I do not think that is likely. I just wish things were as they once were."

Julia gave her friend a sympathetic smile and patted her knee. "Well, I am sorry, dear. I know how fond of him you were."

Rose heaved a sigh of the deeply aggrieved. "I still am, Julia. That is the untoward tragedy of it all."

Rose left her friend's cottage, her mind still filled with thoughts of the dashing Mr. Bowden. She thought of his dark brown hair, with the curl that fell over his forehead in that charming way. She thought of his lovely dark eyes that seemed to hook her in with a glance so that she couldn't look away. She thought of his mouth and all of the wonderfully intelligent things that came out of it. She sighed, feeling mournful. Truthfully, she never did entirely follow all of the intelligent things that Mr. Bowden said. But it was lovely to hear him say them. Was that why he had thrown her over for the far-too-perfect Miss Corley?

She wondered to herself how Miss Corley got to be so disgustingly perfect. Everyone in town was practically in love with Miss Corley. Rose continued to ponder, shamelessly enjoying the self-pity. It stood to reason that Mr. Bowden would inevitably fall under her spell.

Rose stopped. Perhaps that was it! It would explain everything. Perhaps Mr. Bowden had fallen under Miss Corley's *spell*. It was possible that the entire town had fallen under it. She wondered, a bit fretfully, if she had fallen under it too, and grimaced at her recent begrudging praise of the woman.

She put a hand to her cheek. Poor Mr. Bowden! He had fallen in love against his will. She clenched her fist. There was nothing for it. She had to fight back. She had to fight for Mr. Bowden.

READ THE REST OF THE GLAMOUR SPELL OF ROSE TALBOT BY subscribing to Sarah Wallace's newsletter at sarahwallacewriter.com.